Mums and Pumpkin Pie

NETTLES B&B PARA COZY

& COOKBOOK
BOOK THREE

CHRISSY CHICORY
TERESA SEBRING

HALF-PAST 2 PUBLISHING INC.

How This Book Was Baked

*Once upon a time, a lady named Chrissy raised three daughters
on tea, tarts, and fairy tales.
And somewhere not too far away, a culinary dame named
Teresa filled her home with dogs, cats, two sons, and the scent of
something spectacular in the oven.*

*One day, Chrissy's daughter met Teresa's son...
They fell in love, got married, and (in true storybook fashion)
had a beautiful baby girl.
Her name is Briar Rose—and she has two grandmothers who
are completely, wonderfully, hopelessly smitten.*

*One is a Cordon Bleu–trained kitchen sorceress with a knack for
turning seasonal produce into edible poetry.
The other is a weaver of cozy tales who insists every good story
begins with a cup of tea and ends with something sweet.*

*Together, they are Nana Teresa and Nanny Chrissy—a duo
bound by butter, books, and baby giggles.
They write and bake and dream up stories for the people they
love (and occasionally for the pixies who keep stealing their
cinnamon).*

This book is a love letter—to autumn, to flavor, to found family,
and most of all...
to the magic of one little girl who made two grandmothers into
the best kind of teammates.

Prologue

November 29, 1903

The lamps had long since been extinguished. Only the hearth remained aglow, its low, amber light dancing on the polished floorboards of Bithia's parlor. Occasional flashes of heat lightning lit the parlor windows from behind the drawn curtains, the white-blue flicker briefly reflecting across the glossy wood like ghostly footsteps. A thick hush pressed in on the room, broken only by the occasional snap of a log as it settled into embers. The velvet curtains were partially drawn, the fringed tablecloth set precisely beneath the weighted spirit board and planchette. The heady scent of dried roses, wormwood, and clove perfumed the air.

Bithia stood behind the spirit table, her silhouette framed by the firelight. She wore a gown of smoke-gray silk, its high collar fastened with a pearl brooch. Her sleeves were trimmed in antique lace, cuffs buttoned to her narrow wrists. Her hair, the color of tarnished bronze, was swept into a Gibson roll. Severe but elegant. She had the carriage of someone born to a drawing room but shaped by something deeper—by things unseen.

Her sister Cordelia leaned against the parlor's doorframe, half-shrouded in shadow. Her hair was darker, coiled in a glossy chignon that reflected the flickering fire. She wore a deep burgundy walking dress with a velvet sash, and a look that could cut glass. Her lips were pursed, eyes squinched in concentration, every line of her posture rigid with disapproval. Where Bithia exuded mystery, Cordelia held her skepticism like a shield—ever ready, ever sharp.

Bithia adjusted the cuffs of her sleeves, smoothing them out with deliberate grace. Her gaze lingered on the candle, lit not for ambiance but to invite presence. Its flame had flickered strangely all evening, though the windows were shut and the air was still.

There was a knock at the door—three slow, intentional taps. She didn't flinch, having received the letter requesting a meeting with her hours earlier. "Come in, Mr. White," she said, her voice as calm and clear as cut crystal.

The door opened to reveal a hunched figure, shoulders heavy beneath a worn greatcoat that still carried the scent of rain and coal smoke. His face was a landscape of deep furrows, each line carved by sorrow and sleeplessness. Eyes rimmed red and sunken into hollows scanned the room with the haunted look of a man who had seen too much and understood too little of it. His lips were cracked and pale, the corners pulled into a permanent downturn. Every movement he made was stiff, as though his joints were relics of a younger man's body —creaking, halting, uncertain. He stepped inside with the hesitant air of one entering a church or a graveyard. Bithia noted how he clutched something in his right hand, a shape-less bundle wrapped in black silk.

"Thank you for meeting with me," he expressed, his voice as worn and aged as the ancient willow tree outside.

"Please, Mr. White, relax and take a seat," Bithia replied softly, motioning toward the table. "Your note mentioned that you wish to reach out to your son?"

He nodded once, then twice more, as if each time confirmed the truth of it.

She took her place opposite him and closed her eyes.

From the shadows near the hallway, Cordelia's form wavered. Not quite stepping into the light, not quite absent either. Arms crossed, expression sharp. "You know the risks?" she asked softly. "It is no light matter to beg of the dead."

"He comes to release the living," Bithia corrected without opening her eyes.

Cordelia pursed her lips and faded back into the shadows.

The séance began.

Bithia placed her fingertips lightly on the planchette. The board beneath was etched not with letters but with symbols older than English, older than grief. Her breath slowed. The room cooled.

Mr. White placed the silken bundle on the table. It gave a soft thump; not heavy, but wrong. She knew not to look.

"Herbert White," Bithia chanted softly, her voice taking on a rhythmic cadence. "Child of flesh, child of grief, if your spirit remains, we invite you to come closer."

The candle flame danced wildly.

The planchette shifted.

Mr. White gasped. Bithia's voice remained steady.

"Speak, if you will. Or show us what must be known."

The flame flickered, rising and then blazing brightly. In its core, Bithia discerned the silhouette of a young man. He appeared incomplete, unrestful. His face was slightly turned, obscured by the smoke. Behind him, figures came and went in the haze—other faces, other victims. It dawned on her that the monkey's paw had claimed more than just one life.

"He holds me responsible," Mr. White murmured. "I was

the one who made the wish. I brought him back from the dead. But I was afraid."

The flame flickered.

Then the boy in the fire turned completely toward them.

His eyes locked with his father's.

And he nodded.

Just once.

Mr. White broke down. His shoulders trembled, tears streaming silently down his weathered face.

"I was scared," he murmured. "When he returned... there was knocking. I was terrified of what I had done. I wished for it to stop. I wished him away."

Bithia opened her eyes. The fire calmed. The chill retreated.

"He forgives you," she said.

The planchette skidded once more before falling still.

Mr. White reached toward the black silk bundle, his fingers trembling.

"This," he said, unwinding the cloth, "should be burned. I know it. But I—" His voice cracked. "I could not bring myself to do it."

The monkey's paw lay uncovered. It was curled, leathery, and unsettling. Even while still, it seemed conscious. Bithia reached out and wrapped it up again, feeling the faint movement beneath her touch.

"Then leave it with me," she said. "Certain burdens aren't meant to be borne indefinitely."

From the hallway Cordelia exhaled, producing a sound like a hiss. "Shall I escort you out, Mr. White?"

He stood up stiffly, glanced at the fireplace and the paw, then nodded goodbye to Bithia as he followed Cordelia to the door and departed. His heart was still broken, but feeling a bit lighter.

The sisters were alone once more.

"Another relic for the attic?" she inquired.

"Indeed," Bithia confirmed. "With any luck, neglect will lull it to sleep."

She rose, bundle in hand. The candle guttered and went out.

She exited the parlor with deliberate, measured strides. The stairs groaned softly under her as she ascended. At the top, a large room lay shrouded in darkness. Her hand groped through the gloom, locating the locked door. She already had the key in her pocket. The trunk awaited her. It opened with a gentle sigh.

Inside lay a collection of old things wrapped in time and sorrows. A music box, a silver comb, a faded love letter. And now, the paw.

She laid it on velvet. As she closed the lid, the air in the attic seemed to settle. Or brace.

Cordelia, always Bithia's shadow, muttered, "One day, they'll all wake up."

Bithia pressed her palm to the top of the trunk.

"But not tonight," she whispered.

And the key turned, sealing the thing within.

Careful What You Wish For

The scent of cinnamon and cloves wrapped around the Nettles B&B kitchen like a comforter pulled up on a cold morning. Sunshine poured through sheer cream curtains, casting warm golden stripes across the floor and the wide butcher-block island at the center of the room. Butter bubbled in the corners of a cast-iron dish in the oven, where Nan's rosemary sweet potato gratin baked beneath a dusting of nutmeg and sea salt. Its golden scent curled into the kitchen air, mingling with the honey-sweet perfume of freshly clipped mums perched in a chipped pitcher on the windowsill.

She moved with the unhurried grace of someone who had spent a lifetime mastering the ballet of baking. Her white heels clicked in soft punctuation as she swept from bowl to oven, pearls winking at her wrist and a silver chain glinting about her neck. Suspended from that chain, the key nestled just above her heart; warm from skin and memory. A smudge of flour dusted one temple unnoticed, and the corners of her eyes crinkled with purpose as she crimped a pie crust with tidy precision.

Across the kitchen, Mabel's orange floral dress flared like a sunrise each time she bustled past the fridge. Her sandals slapped merrily with every step, and her wild red curls were caught up in a turquoise scarf that she had treasured for decades. She hummed—something jazzy, improvised—as she plunged stems of unruly mums into an old teapot like she was wrangling children into Sunday school clothes. The matching apron she wore was slightly askew, pumpkins on the pocket dancing as she moved.

Together, they looked like a vintage painting given a good shake.

"Pumpkin pies are set, pecan tarts just came out, and the apple-cranberry crisp is bubbling like a potion," Nan announced, sliding the last tart onto the cooling rack with a contented hum. "And if those buckeyes don't set soon—" She frowned, glancing at the rows of peanut butter balls glistening beneath their chocolate caps, lined up like little soldiers across the marble counter.

A flicker of movement caught her eye—just above the fridge, where a pixie wing flashed lavender in the sunlight. Thistle peeked out, clutching a sugar cube the size of his head, only to yelp and vanish as Tansy zipped past in a blur of giggles. Her trailing foot clipped a tin of cinnamon, sending it clattering to the floor in a puff of spice. But Brash was faster than either of them, wings spread wide.

"They're playing hide-and-seek again," Nan muttered, not unkindly. "Poor Thistle doesn't stand a chance."

She wiped her hands on her apron and tilted her head toward the window. The driveway was near empty. The breeze fluttered the curtain edge like a shrug.

"You'd think someone would've shown up by now," she said softly. "Thanksgiving week and only one check-in."

She didn't intend to sound so downhearted, but the house always seemed too silent after the family departed. She and Mossy had hosted the entire extended family before Thanksgiving itself, as it was the only time everyone could free up their schedules. Just two cherished days with the whole family gathered. The highlight of the visit was Sissy, her three-year-old great-granddaughter. Sissy had wandered through the hallways in her berry-stained overalls, shrieking with laughter, leaving a trail of jelly smudges and half-staged tea parties in her wake. The pixies and Mabel's cats hid behind furniture to escape her joyful pursuit. Nan cherished every moment—rocking her after lunch, teaching her to stir cookie dough, and watching her fall asleep holding Buttercup, the worn stuffed bear Nan had once kept on the guest bed purely for decoration.

Being a great-grandmother was nothing short of magic. She once believed nothing could surpass the joy of seeing her daughters grow up, and then her granddaughters, too. But Sissy? Sissy was her heart walking around on the outside.

"I just wish the house were full again," Nan murmured. "Full for Thanksgiving. Full of voices. Full of stories. Full of someone needing another slice of pie."

The words hung in the kitchen like the last notes of a lullaby. Outside, the breeze stirred the flower beds, soft and a little lonely.

Mabel didn't turn. "Maybe they're just late. Maybe they're lost. Maybe they read your Yelp reviews and found out you let gremlins nap in the sugar bowl. Or maybe," she teased as she tucked a mum into the vase with a flourish, "they saw the Tomoka Lights and veered off into the woods, chasing the little sparks into the trees. Happens more than you'd think." She winked at her friend.

From the hallway just beyond the kitchen a faint clink sounded, as if porcelain had shifted on a tray. Nan didn't startle—she simply glanced toward the noise with a soft, knowing smile.

"Bithia?" she called gently. "Cordelia?"

No reply came, but a cool draft slipped into the kitchen, stirring the hem of Nan's skirt.

Mabel shivered. "Tell them if they want pie, they'd best stop spooking around and ask for it like proper guests."

A whisper of rosewater and lavender hung in the air.

Nan adjusted her pearls. "That was them. And I'd venture they consider *us* the guests, not the other way around."

Bithia and Cordelia had come with the house. Or rather, they'd never left. Sisters from the Victorian era, they drifted through the halls and rearranged the furniture at will. Bithia, warm and wistful, often appeared near teacups and candlelight. Cordelia, however, judged with the full force of a withering gaze, especially if the pie crust looked uneven.

Mabel muttered, "Well, one of them needs to learn how to knock."

Nan smirked. "Knock once for yes, twice for no."

A second later the kitchen lights flickered, then both ghosts appeared just beyond the doorway.

Cordelia crossed her arms. "Humor is not your forté."

Nan gave a sweet shrug. "I beg to differ."

Nan smiled at the banter, but her gaze drifted to the refrigerator. A single crayon masterpiece fluttered slightly in the breeze from the cracked window—a bold sun, three teacups, and a vaguely bear-shaped blob with pink bows. Sissy's name was scrawled across the bottom in Nan's own handwriting, all proud loops and loving curves.

She murmured, almost to herself:

"In a parlor warm with morning light,
  Marshmallow Bears sat pink and white…"

Mabel looked up. "What was that, dear?"

4

"Oh, nothing." Nan touched the corner of the paper with her fingertip. "Just the start of a poem in my head, that's all."

Mabel pointed a mum-stained finger at her. "Then you had better get to your writing desk before it flies off with the pixies."

"It's already halfway to the parlor," Nan said with a heavy heart, frowning. "I just wish the house would be full for Thanksgiving." Just then, something latched onto the back of her ankle.

Cool. Leathery. Deliberate.

A flash of lightning lit up the kitchen like a camera going off. The cheerful sun disappeared as dark clouds rolled in fast and sudden, as if summoned. Wind slammed against the side of the house, rattling the windows. One of them, left cracked open, yawned wider with a gust, sending the lace curtain flapping like a frantic flag.

Nan jerked and turned, heart stuttering. "Mabel, did you see what just touched me?"

Mabel spun, eyes wide. "Forget that! Help me shut this window before the mums fly to Georgia!"

Before Nan could move, something scuttled from beneath the table—fast, jointed, wrong.

"Mouse!" Mabel shrieked.

"That was no mouse!" Nan grabbed the rolling pin with one hand and her resolve with the other. "It had fingers."

"Oh, well, that makes it better."

A blur of withered brown shot across the floor, curving toward the stove with alarming speed. It wasn't just moving. It *knew* where it was going.

Mabel lunged for the broom. "It's Thing from the Addams Family! It's Thing and it's in your kitchen!"

"Not on Thanksgiving weekend!" Nan hollered, brandishing her rolling pin like a saber. "It must have escaped from the attic. *That* room."

"The one you swore you'd clean out in March?"

"Yes, well, it's self-emptying now. And apparently self-propelled."

The paw disappeared under the island. Flour sacks trembled. Then toppled.

A white cloud exploded across the kitchen.

Mabel emerged from the fog, coughing. "That's it. I'm calling an exterminator. Or a priest. Maybe both."

Bithia hovered just above the floorboards like a ribbon of smoke. Her skirts drifted slightly as if caught in a breeze no one else could feel. She didn't speak at first, only turned—her translucent form pivoting to follow the paw's path with eyes wide and troubled.

"Oh dear," she murmured. "I had hoped never to see *that* object again."

Cordelia flickered into sharper view beside her, arms already crossed, lips drawn tight with disapproval. She had been hovering near the pantry, watching. Waiting. The moment the paw had scuttled across the floor, she'd flinched back as if slapped.

"This," she growled, voice low and curling like fog, "is *exactly* why we lock that door." Her eyes drifted to the key around Nan's neck.

Three shrill cackles sliced through the haze.

The pixies.

They streaked through the pantry door, trailing sparks and giggles like caffeinated confetti. With a gleeful cry, they grabbed hold of the monkey paw and hauled it into the air like an absurd parade float.

"It's a demonic chicken foot!" Mabel bellowed, swinging her broom like a desperate drum major.

Nan chased after them, her rolling pin high. "You are not welcome here! Go back to the attic! I mean it!"

The pixies swerved toward the mudroom. The paw slipped from their grip, twirling end over end.

The doggy door flapped.

And it was gone.

Just then, Nan noticed the boy who had stepped into the kitchen. He wore a too-big coat, scuffed sneakers that lit up with every step, and a look of pure, delighted curiosity.

He paused. Took it all in—the flour-drenched women, the chaos, the open doggy door.

"That," he said, blinking behind thick glasses, "was *awesome*."

"How long have you been standing there?" asked Nan.

"Long enough," the boy replied, shrugging.

Nan exhaled. "Mabel, meet Ollie. He and his family are here for Thanksgiving. They checked in last night."

He nodded. His cheeks were pink from the excitement, and his hair curled like question marks. He clutched a battered notebook.

"I saw it last night, too," he said, flipping through pages. "Thought it was a weasel. Definitely wasn't."

"You're not scared?" Mabel asked, astounded.

Ollie grinned. "Of that? No way. I want to trap it. I think it grants wishes. Probably not nice ones, by the look of it. But still."

He flipped open his notebook and pointed to a scribble that he crossed out and re-labeled *Monkey Paw-ish Thing?? Cursed?*

"I read a spooky story once about one—creepy old tale. My dad said it was made up, but I don't think so. This one feels... real."

Mabel blinked. "Well, this child understands this house."

"Children usually do," Nan murmured, crouching to his level. "What would you wish for?"

He tilted his head, thoughtful. "Teleportation. A dragon. And for my little sister to stop deleting my saved games."

Mabel chuckled. "You've got your priorities straight. I admire that. Here, have a cookie." Ollie took it in his hand, then quietly moved to the doggy door and peered outside.

The backyard was still, but the sky above had shifted. Dark clouds now gathered like gossip.

"I think it'll come back," he murmured.

Nan touched the key at her chest. It was warm again.

"So do I."

Ollie opened his notebook. Beneath a scribbled drawing of a clawed foot, he wrote:

Subject: Monkey Paw. Possibly cursed. Definitely fast. Extremely cool.

Nan rose and dusted herself off. "Let's clean this up. We've got guests coming."

Mabel blinked. "We do?"

The phone rang.

Nan didn't answer right away. Her eyes were on the doggie door.

She smiled.

"We do now."

Forecast- Full House

Mossy stood in the center of the foyer like a man preparing to direct aircraft on a flooded runway. His cardigan pockets bulged oddly—one held a flashlight with a duct-taped handle, the other a bundle of extra guest keys. Around his neck hung a twine-laced whistle, which he blew periodically with great gravity despite the fact that no one was listening. A clipboard was tucked under his arm, covered in looping script and faint doodles of constellations. He used it to assign rooms with the fervor of a man matching travelers to their destined stars.

The storm had arrived in full, sweeping down from the ocean with tropical flair and the dramatics of a Shakespearean lead. Towels soaked with rainwater lined the entry floor, squelching with every footstep. The old grandfather clock in the corner ticked unbothered, though even it seemed to wince with every crack of thunder.

"Rooms to the left of the stair are better for Aquarians," Mossy was telling the bewildered guests. "They're dreamers. But if you're a Capricorn I recommend the blue room on the second floor—it's got a stoic little desk and a solid view of the side yard. Suits that temperament."

He blew the whistle once, pointed the flashlight dramatically toward the staircase, and gestured up like he was taxiing toward a runway gate.

"Order, elegance, and scotch," Mossy muttered to himself, marking something down. "We must maintain them all."

A crash sounded as the front door blew open again, bringing with it two figures and a small cascade of leaves and rain.

"Well if it isn't the hurricane in technicolor," Mossy said with a grin.

The Shapiro Sisters entered in what could only be described as a coordinated gale. Mildred wore a neon pink skort, a zippered windbreaker with fluorescent yellow piping, and a glittered visor that somehow managed to stay perfectly dry. Her paddle was holstered at her side like a sheriff's revolver. Gladys trailed behind in leopard-print leggings, a bedazzled hoodie that read *Pickle Queen*, and a fanny pack strapped with military precision.

"We came prepared," Mildred announced.

Gladys sneezed. "Does it smell like cinnamon or lemonade in here?"

Mossy smiled serenely. "We steep both into the experience. Welcome back, ladies."

Mildred peeled off her windbreaker with flair. "We've never missed a pickleball tournament in ten years, not even during that one in Fort Lauderdale where the courts flooded and Gladys played in galoshes."

"If memory serves me, they called you the Paddle Pirate," Mossy said with a solemn nod. "Legendary."

"We've also never lost," Gladys added, shaking out her hoodie like a matador preparing for battle. "Ever. Not once. Undefeated."

"Until now," came Rufus's voice through a mouthful of biscuit. He was leaning on the banister, crumbs dotting his shirt. "Moss and I have been training. Watching videos. Stretching. Eating smart."

"You ate four pumpkin tarts and two sausage rolls before breakfast," Nan called from the kitchen.

"That's my carb load," Rufus said proudly.

Mildred crossed her arms. "You boys are goin' down."

"Like overcooked soufflés," Gladys chimed.

Mossy blew a puff of air through his pursed lips. "We shall meet you upon the courts, not as mere mortals but as titans of turf. As Pindar wrote: 'Unsung, the noblest deed will die.'"

There was a long pause.

"Is that, like, code for 'bring it'?" Gladys asked.

"I think it means we're gonna win," Rufus translated.

Mossy winked. "That's the spirit."

As they tromped toward the coat rack, the front parlor gave a sudden metallic clink—like piano keys tapping gently beneath a hand.

Mossy's eyes narrowed. He turned slightly, peering through the open doorway.

Cordelia sat primly at the old upright piano, her gloved fingers gliding over the keys in perfect form. She did not meet his gaze, but her chin rose slightly in defiance.

He cleared his throat. "Madam, might I request quiet amid the storm?"

Cordelia vanished like mist caught in a sunbeam.

Rufus appeared in her place a moment later, mouth full of biscuit. "Who're you talkin' to, Moss?"

"No one who listens," Mossy said. "Which makes two of you."

From the hallway, the scent of cinnamon and apple wafted in like a peace offering. Nan appeared with a tray of teacups, followed closely by Mabel, who carried a tin of cheese biscuits and a dish towel that appeared to have been recently weaponized.

Mabel swatted at a flash of lavender and gold as it buzzed past. "Pixie!" she whined. "Get your crumb-snatching paws off those croissants; yours are in the kitchen!"

"Pixies?" Kiki asked, stepping into the room with her phone held aloft. She wore a lemon-yellow raincoat and matching boots, her fiancé Brent in tow with an umbrella and the weariness of a man who'd driven through soup.

"They're mostly harmless," Nan assured. "And somewhat fond of apricots."

Kiki raised an eyebrow. "I was just reading your reviews. Did you know someone claims to have seen a haunted crab claw in your laundry chute?"

"Ah, yes," Mossy said, not missing a beat. "Sebastian. Bit of a diva."

Brent blinked. "It's flooding out there. We had to swerve around a kayak on Main Street."

"You're staying then," Mossy said matter-of-factly. "Power's out east of Ridgewood. You'll find our generator surprisingly polite." He turned toward the staircase and raised his clipboard like a conductor. "You can have our room. Nan, we'll be in the Mossy Mobile tonight."

Nan reappeared in the archway with a tray of cider and raised a brow. "You gave away our bed?"

"We are full to the brim." Mossy smiled over the rim of his glasses. "Fear not, my love. I foresee a romantic night under the willow tree. The radio for ambiance. Rain on the roof. Possibly a thermos of mulled wine if I can find where you've hidden it."

Nan tilted her head, visibly amused. "As long as it's not the polka station again."

"I make no promises."

She handed him a cup of cider and let her fingers linger. The Mossy Mobile was their RV, parked beneath the sweeping arms of the weeping willow in the backyard. A cozy little retreat where they'd weathered more than one storm with music and mismatched socks.

"You and me and the rain," she said, voice softening.

"And maybe Cordelia peeking through the window," he added with mock horror.

"Then she can bring her own wine."

Kiki glanced at her phone. "Another guest said there was unexplained music coming from the parlor."

"Was it Chopin?" Mossy asked, already flipping a page on his clipboard. "Cordelia's partial to nocturnes."

"Cordelia is your...?"

"She is a bit of a traditionalist."

Kiki blinked. "Right."

Rufus coughed loudly and inhaled a tart.

Thunder rolled across the roof like bowling balls. A window near the stairwell rattled and Mossy immediately turned to it, flashlight raised like a sword.

"Withstand me not, foul draft!" he cried, fishing plastic sheeting from a basket by the door. "We shall endure!"

He taped it with one hand while quoting, "Blow, winds, and crack your cheeks!"

Mabel muttered behind him. "He's gone full King Lear. Someone hide the whiskey."

Nan handed her a tray. "Help me freshen the tea before he builds an ark."

The guests clustered in the sitting area, peeling off wet layers and clutching mismatched teacups. Towels were distributed like offerings. Somewhere upstairs, a music box played a few haunting notes before falling silent again.

Mabel froze mid-pour, eyes wide. "Was that *the* music box?"

Nan didn't even glance up. "No, not that one. It's just the old one in the blue room—it plays when the radiator kicks in."

Mabel exhaled, setting the teapot down with a thud. "Okay. Because if *that* thing's back, I'm sleeping in my car."

"You didn't drive here."

"Then I'll borrow Cordelia's favorite chaise."

Nan smirked. "You really think she'd share?"

From the corner of the parlor, a chill drifted across the floor. Cordelia floated just at the edge of the doorway, arms crossed, one eyebrow raised as if to say *excuse me?*

Mabel squinted at her. "Don't give me that look."

Cordelia gave a long blink then vanished, her skirts trailing behind her like smoke caught in a draft.

Nan sipped her cinnamon apple tea.

From the landing, Bithia appeared just long enough to meet Mossy's eyes.

He tipped his head respectfully then turned back to the crowd.

"Ladies and gentlemen," Mossy called, lifting his whistle again. "Welcome to the Nettles B&B. Your refuge from storm, power outage, and possibly reality."

The guests clapped, unsure why.

Mabel leaned close to Nan. "Well, your wish came true. The B&B is filled to the brim for Thanksgiving."

"Nonsense. This wasn't me." Nan whispered. "Florida weather does her own thing."

"Uh-huh." Mabel narrowed her eyes as another pixie darted past. "And what about that chicken foot scuttling under the loveseat earlier?"

Nan handed her a biscuit. "Monkey paw, if Ollie is correct."

Thunder cracked again—and from the kitchen came a faint, unmistakable clatter.

It was back.

But for now, everyone had tea. And Mossy still had the whistle.

Wishes and Whispers

The banister creaked like a lazy accordion as a parade of small feet clambered down the stairs. Bea, Ollie's younger sister, skipped the last two steps and landed in a giggle. She wore a bright red sundress and matching red galoshes, her blond curls bouncing with each step. Around five years old, Bea radiated unfiltered joy and mischief.

Ollie followed close behind, clutching a small notepad and a pencil as if on official duty. He was eight, tall for his age, with a shock of untamable brown hair and a pair of glasses that perpetually slid down his nose. He had changed into a buttoned vest over his T-shirt and had tucked a magnifying glass into his pocket. Every inch of him said 'detective at work'.

Nan, carrying a tray of blue and white tea cups toward the kitchen, paused just long enough to smile. The house felt warmer with children in it, their laughter softening the edges of the storm outside.

"You go first," Bea whispered to Ollie. "Wish for something cool!"

Ollie adjusted his notepad. "I wish it wasn't raining. I wanted to learn how to play pickleball with Rufus."

Bea clapped her hands. "I wish for two cookies instead of one."

Nan, now returning from the kitchen with a towel over her shoulder, overheard and slowed. The words were sweet and innocent, a chorus of wishes rising above the scent of cinnamon and storm.

And then it happened.

Bea darted down the stairs toward the rug to retrieve a fallen ball—only to trip, yelp, and tumble softly into Ollie. Something brown and knobby skittered away beneath the umbrella stand.

"Did you see that?" Ollie cried, scrambling to his feet.

Bea rubbed her knee. "It was like... a creepy root with claws!"

Nan hurried forward, crouching beside them. "Everyone all right?"

Ollie nodded, but his eyes narrowed toward the shadows. "That thing again. I'm gonna catch it. I have a plan."

Bea leaned in and whispered, "It looked like it was listening to us. When we were wishing."

Before Nan could answer Susan appeared at the top of the stairs, steady and smiling. "What are we wishing for now, my munchkins?"

Bea pointed. "Mommy, I wished for more cookies."

Ollie shouted, "I wished for wings!"

Susan chuckled as she descended. "Wishing is wonderful, isn't it? Childhood should be full of it. But since it's Thanksgiving week, how about a little of wishing's cousin, gratitude? What are we grateful for instead?"

Bea wrinkled her nose but thought about it. "I'm grateful for bears."

Ollie, still scribbling in his notepad, said, "I'm grateful for mysteries. And secret passageways. And pie, too."

Susan smiled. "Those are lovely things to be grateful for,"

she said in a soft voice. "I'll go see how your dad is doing. Try not to get into too much mischief." She gave Bea's curls a light ruffle, then turned and headed upstairs. "Tom, do you need any help with the unpacking?" she called out as she climbed the stairs.

Nan lingered for a moment, watching the kids return to their wishful game. Her gaze drifted toward the parlor, where an unfamiliar guest sat alone with a cooling cup of tea. Eleanor, she thought her name was. Quiet. Tired-looking. She hadn't said much since arriving. A faint hum drifted from her direction—not a tune Nan recognized, but lullaby-soft.

Just as Nan took a step toward her, the air shifted.

A flicker of movement. A blur of wings. The pixies burst through the hallway like a rogue marching band, cackling and hollering, holding the monkey paw aloft like it was the trophy from a very strange scavenger hunt.

Nan gasped. " Oh, be careful!"

The paw glinted, clenched in Thistle's small but mighty grip while Tansy clung to his leg; her wings beating double-time while steering like she was directing a sled. Bitter held up the weight of the middle, glitter raining down from his wings. They zipped straight through the parlor—right past Eleanor, who stilled but didn't look up—and into the stairwell, disappearing like a flash of static.

Nan made to follow but paused.

Eleanor was humming again. Low. Heart-deep.

Nan listened, hand stilling on the banister. She didn't know the tune, but she recognized the weight behind it. Grief had a sound. Longing did, too.

She would speak to her later. For now, she let the quiet remain.

A tiny voice spoke behind her.

"Miss Nan," Bea said, tugging on her apron. "Can we have a tea party with the bear?"

Nan followed the girl's gaze. Buttercup. She crouched beside a large basket she'd tucked by the pantry. Inside were a few beloved things Nan had gathered for Sissy: a tin tea set, a lace-edged bib, and Buttercup—a fuzzy teddy bear, bow-bedecked and slightly worn.

Nan plucked the bear free and brushed a crumb from its ear. "Her name is Buttercup. She's hosted many fine teas. Think she'd be happy to join yours?"

Bea nodded solemnly. "She looks like she tells good stories."

Nan smiled and handed her the bear. "She does. Especially when there's pumpkin pie involved."

Ollie appeared with his notebook. "I'm writing it all down. Everything the paw does. I'm calling it *Paw Watch*. Capital P. Capital W."

"Excellent," Nan said. "I feel much safer with you on duty, young Ollie."

The boy nodded seriously and dashed off toward the stairs.

Nan stood there a moment longer, watching as Bea settled into the parlor with Buttercup, setting the tea things with surprising care. The house, for all its creaks and currents, felt deeply alive.

And in the doorway, half-seen, the pixies hovered for just a beat—glancing once toward Eleanor, as if sensing something silent and sad. Then they vanished up the stairs with Ollie on their heels, his laughter trailing like a paper kite in the wind.

Nan exhaled and turned back toward the kitchen, a line of verse already forming in her mind.

She would write it down, soon. Before the pixies carried that thought away, too.

 The Pickleball Prophecy

The door to Mossy's study was firmly shut, as if the storm outside might have the audacity to interrupt the rituals within. Rain tapped against the windowpanes in a rhythm that sounded suspiciously like a metronome set for dramatic flair.

Inside, Mossy stood beside a chalkboard he'd wheeled in from the garage, on which he'd carefully illustrated a series of pickleball court diagrams. At the top, written in florid calligraphy, were the words: *Pickleball: A Philosophical Primer for Gentlemen of Courage.*

Rufus slumped in a leather armchair that had seen better decades. He munched on a slice of Nan's banana bread and eyed Mossy with the wide, uncertain stare of someone who knew they were about to be dragged into something significant—and possibly ridiculous.

"Let me be clear," Mossy said, tapping the chalkboard with a wooden pointer. "These are not ordinary opponents. They are The Shapiro Sisters."

Rufus swallowed loudly. "Right. And they're... sisters."

"Indeed." Mossy paced. "They eat dinks for breakfast. Their serves are as sharp as satire. Mildred once broke a paddle on purpose—just to intimidate an umpire. Gladys hasn't smiled since Reagan's first term."

Rufus blinked. "Are they... hot in action?"

Mossy raised an eyebrow. "They are... formidable."

Rufus shifted uneasily. "You mean hot."

"No," Mossy said serenely. "I mean terrifying."

A bolt of lightning cracked the sky, briefly illuminating the room in stark white. The lights flickered. Mossy didn't flinch.

From the parlor down the hall came a chorus of voices, low and rhythmic.

"Hydrate or die-drate!" bellowed a voice.

Rufus jumped. "What the—was that Mildred?"

"They're warming up," Mossy said, peeking through the door. "Coordinated stretching. Deep lunges. Gladys just did a toe-touch and made it look like a threat."

"I'm not ready for this," Rufus muttered.

Mossy sipped his tea. "No one ever is."

Rufus stood and began doing slow windmills with his arms. "Okay. Okay. I can work with this. You're my coach. We can make a game plan. We'll outwit them. Outspeed them. Outsass them."

"And pray for mercy," Mossy added helpfully.

The room smelled of aged books, lemon furniture polish, and the faintest trace of Nan's lavender cookies. Mossy's desk was cluttered with old manuscripts and an antique globe that always spun northward no matter how it was turned.

Lightning flashed again, briefly illuminating something on the floor.

Tap.

Scraaaatch.

Tap tap.

Rufus looked down. "What's that sound?"

Mossy leaned slightly, listening. "Perhaps the house is

settling. Or the pixies are practicing rhythmic gymnastics. You never know with them."

The sound skittered closer, then vanished.

Rufus dropped into the leather chair once more, cradling a tumbler of whisky. As he sank in, he sighed, "I wish we could beat them at the tournament. I really want to win."

The words were barely out of his mouth when he yelped. "YOWCH! Something just goosed me!"

He shot upright, the whisky sloshing across the armrest and into the shadows below. A small, leathery shape darted from under the cushion and disappeared into the bookcase.

"I think the chair is haunted," Rufus said, one hand rubbing the spot where something had jabbed him.

Mossy crouched by the spill. "Or perhaps it merely holds a grudge."

Rufus rubbed his backside. "Seriously, Moss. That felt like a claw. Or a gnarled... something."

Mossy tilted his head. "The house is old. It's prone to quirks. That was likely just a trick of the upholstery."

Outside the window, three pixies hurriedly flew by. Tansy, one of them, carried a small lasso made of twine and a button. Thistle navigated with wild carelessness as Neat shouted strategic directions.

"Are the pixies... chasing something?" Rufus asked.

"Likely a sugar cube," Mossy said. "Or destiny. They chase both with equal enthusiasm."

A knock sounded at the study door.

Mabel cautiously peered in, holding a tray of snacks. "I've got peppermints and pretzels. But if that claw-footed gremlin is here, I'm not coming inside." She scanned the room, noticing a whisky stain on a chair, and squinted suspiciously.

"What gremlin?" Rufus inquired.

She placed the peppermints on the nearest table and

retreated. "Something escaped from the trunk upstairs. The current theory is it's a monkey paw that grants wishes."

"Really, Mabel," Mossy remarked, carefully picking out a mint. "That's quite intriguing."

"Just wait until you see it before you decide," she replied as she left the room.

Once she was out, Rufus turned to Mossy.

"Okay. Hypothetically. Let's say I made a wish. Right when the claw-throne jabbed me. And the Sisters lose. That's good, right? We win. Glory. Maybe matching jackets."

Mossy frowned. "Did you say it aloud? The wish?"

Rufus nodded. "Yup. Said it right into the chair."

A gust of wind slammed against the window. The candle on Mossy's desk flickered. Somewhere beyond the study, a music box played three slow, eerie notes.

Mossy rose, hands behind his back. "Well, then. That complicates things."

"Should I cancel the wish?" Rufus asked.

"One rarely cancels a wish," Mossy murmured. "But one can outwit it."

The monkey paw darted across the floor again, chased by pixies who were now armed with ribbon and a cork.

Mossy pointed dramatically with his flashlight. "Halt, cursed talon! You trespass in a house of literature and cinnamon tea!"

The paw ignored him, vanishing into the vent with a final scritch.

Rufus sank back into the chair. "Did we just cast a spell?"

"Possibly," Mossy said. "Or doomed ourselves to a karmic pickleball showdown. Both are exciting."

Rufus clutched his towel like a security blanket. "Remind me again, why are we doing this?"

Mossy handed him a headband embroidered with tiny

literary quotes. "Because, dear Rufus, some stories choose us. Now hydrate, stretch, and prepare for the Shapiropocalypse."

From the next room, a shout:

"Gladys, adjust your grip! We're aiming for domination, not decorum!"

Rufus whimpered. "If I perish, tell the world I died chasing greatness."

Mossy lifted his teacup. "To valiant absurdity."

The wind howled. The paw twitched somewhere in the shadows. The second wish had been made.

And the house, as always, was listening.

Pixie Games & Kitchen Chaos

The storm hadn't let up. Wind howled through the chimney, and rain slapped the windowpanes with the occasional insult. But inside the kitchen, it was its own brand of chaos—warm, wild, and lightly powdered with sugar.

Nan reached for the teapot just as something zipped past her head. A flash of glitter, a giggle, and the copper ladle fell with a clang.

"Tansy!" she called, exasperated but not unkind. "Leave the utensils alone. They are not weapons."

Thistle and Tansy were in rare form. The pixies darted through the kitchen, wings shimmering in the soft light. Between them, suspended like a football in flight, dangled the monkey paw. It twisted midair as if trying to escape their clutches.

From the hallway came thunderous footsteps.

"I saw it!" Ollie declared, notebook clutched to his chest, pencil behind one ear. "It went this way!"

Bea tumbled in behind him, squealing in delight as she spotted the paw. "It has toes! Ew, I love it!"

Nan side-stepped as the children stormed past, nearly

knocking over a tray of unbaked rolls. "Slow down, darlings. That thing is not a toy."

Mabel, from her corner of flower arrangement duty, didn't even flinch. "Let 'em run. Builds character. And burns off the cookies."

Nan wiped her hands on a dish towel. "I've started tracking its movements. The paw."

Mabel arched a brow. "You have a chart?"

Nan gestured to a sticky note collage beside the spice rack. "Kitchen. Study. Parlor. Dining room. And always right before something odd happens."

"Darling," Mabel said with a chuckle, plucking a peach-toned rose from her basket, "everything around here is odd. You could pin the tail on the weird and hit the mark."

Nan leaned against the counter. "Still... what does the paw want? Do you think it truly grants wishes, like Ollie suggested?"

Mabel shook out the folds of a new tea towel, then set about trimming the stem of her latest bloom. "Fine. You be Miss Marple. I'll be Miss Mabel. And this Miss Mabel would like a rose the color of early peaches. Not too pink, not too orange. Fragrant. Lush. The kind of rose that could survive a summer rain without falling apart."

"That's a very specific rose," Nan said.

"It is." Mabel sighed dreamily. "And if wishes are to be granted, that's mine. Just one. A perfect peach rose in my garden."

Nan grinned. "That sentiment belongs in the guest book."

"I'd rather carve it into reality," Mabel said.

Just then the monkey paw, midflight between pixie paws, slammed directly into Mabel's shoulder.

"Ow!" she cried. "Rude!"

It hit the floor and skittered under the table as Bea dove after it.

"It touched you," Nan said softly.

Mabel blinked. "So? I wasn't wishing when it touched me."

Nan just gave her a long look. "I suppose you're right."

Before Mabel could reply, a soft throat-clearing came from the doorway.

Eleanor stood there with her teacup, empty and politely held. She was dressed in a soft gray cardigan over a navy blouse, her dark hair loosely twisted at the nape.

Nan immediately stepped forward. "Let me warm that up for you."

"Thank you," Eleanor said, her voice barely above the hush of the rain. She glanced at the window. "Do you think the storm will pass by tomorrow?"

"Hard to say," Mabel replied, gentle for once. "Florida weather likes to make an entrance, then linger like a guest that won't take a hint."

Eleanor managed a soft smile. "My daughter always loved the rain. When she was young, she would say it sounded like fairy feet on the roof."

Nan recognized that look: the practiced smile, the headache hiding behind the eyes.

"She's... in the hospital," Eleanor explained. "There was a car accident. The doctor I spoke with on the phone informed me that she's in a coma. I was headed there when all the flights got canceled."

Mabel and Nan exchanged a glance, the moment weighted.

"She's strong," Eleanor continued. "And funny. A little sarcastic. She'd probably prefer I stayed here drinking tea, pretending everything's fine. But I can't. I can't stand the thought of her being there alone."

Nan gently passed her a fresh cup. "I'm so sorry, Eleanor. Really."

Eleanor nodded, murmured her thanks, and disappeared back down the hall.

Silence held for a moment.

They were still for a long breath, until a crash from the top of the stairs and a squeal from Ollie sent them both moving again.

Mabel raised her broom. "Pixies or paw, your reign ends now!"

The Wader Brigade

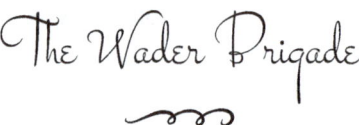

The rain had no intention of stopping. It came sideways now, in gusts and sheets, turning gutters into rivers and the road in front of the B&B into something that could reasonably accommodate a canoe. Which, as it happened, someone was already testing.

Mossy peered out the front door and squinted through his bifocals. "Is that...a Coleman canoe?"

Rufus, standing behind him and juggling two croissants, leaned in. "They've got beer."

A sunburned couple in sleeveless tees floated by, each with a Coors Light in hand, the woman waving cheerfully through the deluge.

"Indeed they do." Mossy saluted with his flashlight. "Fair winds, noble mariners!"

The man raised his can in salute. "Goes where it goes, brother!"

Mabel bustled in from the back hallway, carrying a bundle of towels.

It was clear the storm had turned from inconvenient to absurd, and Mossy was prepared. He had spent the better part of the morning laying out what he called "The Expedition Gear" in the foyer: a row of fishing waders, motorcycle helmets left over from the previous Bike Week, a rainproof clipboard, and a flashlight with fresh batteries. Over his sweatshirt he had added a bright yellow slicker, now dramatically cinched at the waist.

Rufus hooted. "It's on like Donkey Kong!"

Mossy adjusted the helmet on his head—the one with a pink glitter visor. "Pictona awaits. The bracket begins at two. We march."

"Swim," Rufus muttered, but he took the offered helmet and a pair of waders with a resigned sigh.

Just then, the Shapiro Sisters descended the staircase like an army of one. Mildred led the charge in lime green spandex, her skort flaring like a battle flag. Gladys followed, navy skort perfectly pressed, paddle slung across her back like a sword.

"It's time!" Mildred barked.

Rufus stared, croissant halfway to his mouth. "Are they...? Traveling with us?"

Mossy didn't miss a beat. "We escort them to their demise."

The sisters inspected the waders. Mildred grunted. "These don't breathe."

Gladys pulled hers on with a snap. "Neither do we when we play."

Mabel returned, dropping towels at the front door like sandbags. She eyed the assembled crew with mock solemnity. "Is this what we've come to? Pictona's last stand?"

Nan appeared behind her, arms folded, a dish towel tossed over her shoulder. "It looks like a cross between a disaster relief squad and the Village People."

Mossy offered a gallant bow. "We go not for glory but for honor. And perhaps a shiny gold trophy."

Nan suppressed a grin. "Don't drown, Mossy dear."

Mabel handed Rufus a paper bag. "Nan made ham and cheddar scones. They're still warm."

Rufus clutched the bag like it was life-saving cargo. "You're angels in aprons."

Nan handed Mossy a thermos. "Ginger tea. For courage."

Mossy pressed his hand to his heart. "You send us forth like knights from the Round Table."

They stepped out into the deluge like a poorly dressed parade. Mossy led the way, with Rufus trailing behind and the sisters bringing up the rear.

The journey to Pictona was less a march and more a slow-motion ballet of splashes, muttered curses, and dodging floating debris. Rufus kept yelling, "Is that lightning or an omen?!" every time the sky flashed. Mossy, meanwhile, led with the gravitas of a man reenacting the exploration of the Amazon.

"Take heart, comrades! If Sir Percy Fawcett could brave the jungle seeking the Lost City of Z, surely we can navigate to a covered pickleball court!"

Mildred muttered, "This is Florida, not El Dorado."

Rufus stopped dead. "GATOR!"

Screaming erupted as Gladys launched herself onto Mossy like a startled cat. He staggered back into a flooded bush.

"That is a branch," Mossy gasped, flailing. "A slightly aggressive one, granted, but wood nonetheless."

Gladys clung to his shoulders. "Well, I wasn't taking any chances!"

Rufus poked the object with his paddle. "Yep. Definitely a stick. Possibly driftwood. But definitely not carnivorous."

They trudged on.

A pair of teens on paddleboards passed them near the intersection of Ridgewood and Palmetto, tossing peace signs and listening to music through a waterproof speaker. The soundtrack of their journey became a bizarre mix of Fleetwood Mac and rumbling thunder.

By the time they reached Pictona, the courts were wet but not flooded. A line of determined players had already formed under a sturdy canopy. A young volunteer in a poncho was handing out hot cocoa.

Mossy looked at Rufus—rain-soaked, helmet-headed, and completely bewildered.

"Sir," he said solemnly, "we have crossed rivers in waders, battled phantom gators, and survived the shrieks of Amazonian women in neon spandex. We did not come all this way for mere recreation. No. Like all grand adventurers, we came in pursuit of something greater—honor, glory... and perhaps a commemorative mug."

Rufus sniffed, nodding gravely. "Let's dink for destiny."

Mildred blew her whistle. "Game on!"

Sugar, Spice, and Softening Hearts

Rain thrummed against the windows in a steady, contemplative rhythm, like a lullaby hummed by the house itself. The parlor was a soft glow of lamplight and candle flicker, a sanctuary of warmth against the gray drizzle outside. Nan had set the scene just so: a vinyl of Debussy waltzed gently on the gramophone, the Blue Willow teapot sat steaming beside plates of pumpkin scones, and the fireplace snapped and sighed as if content with its current company.

Bea, resplendent in a paper crown studded with crayon hearts and the occasional gluey pom-pom, galloped across the rug with her napkin cape flying behind her. "I dub thee Sir Ollie the Brave!" she declared, tapping her brother's shoulder with a butter knife.

Ollie, clipboard still tucked under one arm, accepted the title solemnly. His own crown was more of a tactical helmet, complete with a sketched monkey paw trap diagram scrawled on one side and a list of potential wish outcomes on the other.

Nan perched on the edge of the tufted settee, her apron still dusted with flour. One hand was wrapped around a paper-thin teacup, the other flicked a strand of hair from her brow as she watched the scene unfold.

"Every good knight needs a battle tune," she said, and gave the gramophone a gentle nudge to the next track—something soft and string-heavy that made Bea spin like a ballerina.

On the table nearby, several pixies snored gently in sugar bowls. Neat had curled into a powdered sugar drift like a kitten, while Brash had draped himself over a cube like a fainting Victorian. A single sneeze from Brash dusted the lace doily with a puff of sweetness.

Bea saw, and gasped in delight. "That one sneezed! That means he's dreaming of knights and castles!"

Ollie narrowed his eyes. "Or he has allergies. They are bad this time of year, you know."

Nan smiled at the children, then turned to collect empty plates from the low tea table. As she passed Eleanor's chair, she paused.

The woman's teacup was half-filled and precariously perched on the arm of her chair; her other hand rested on a closed book in her lap. The room buzzed with activity and noise. The children were playing loudly. Kiki and Brent were by the fireplace, making videos. Despite this, Eleanor felt like the calm center of the chaos. Her gray cardigan was snug around her shoulders, and her bun had started to unravel at the nape of her neck. Her eyes wandered to the children and she gave a faint smile at Bea's latest announcement, but her grip on the teacup tightened once more.

From the edge of the curtain, Cordelia floated silently. Her form was outlined just barely by the lamplight, a Victorian specter in a high-collared gown. Her arms were folded, her expression unreadable.

Bithia appeared beside her, more shimmer than substance, her attention torn between the children and her sister.

Nan saw them both. She did not speak. Just offered the smallest nod and returned to her seat.

"Miss Nan," Bea said, suddenly solemn, "do the pixies live in the sugar bowls all the time?"

Nan chuckled. "Oh, only when it rains. They don't like getting their wings soggy."

"Do they go to sleep when it's sunny?"

"Of course not," Ollie said, rolling his eyes. "They sunbathe on the windowsill and steal ice cubes from lemonade."

Tansy stirred, gave a sleepy hiccup, and rolled over in the sugar bowl.

Bea clapped joyfully and dipped her hand into a basket at her feet, rummaging through assorted trinkets. She pulled out the soft, butter-yellow teddy bear with the slightly crooked ear and a child's hair ribbon. She embraced it as if it had always belonged to her.

"How is Buttercup?" Nan inquired gently.

Bea tilted her head and beamed with joy. "You're right. She's good at tea parties."

Mabel entered, carrying a fresh tray of cinnamon scones, and paused to take in the scene—children crowned, pixies snoring, ghosts observing, and Nan softly humming along to the record.

She put the tray down and nudged Thistle back into his bowl. "Sugar hog. You left none for the rest of us."

Cordelia stepped forward just as Eleanor stood.

Nan moved to refill her cup.

"Still raining," Eleanor murmured, eyes on the storm. "But this room doesn't seem to mind."

"This house never does," Nan said. "It just leans into whatever season comes."

Cordelia hovered behind Eleanor, her head tilted. She

reached out as if to touch her shoulder but stopped, her hand curling into a fist.

Nan noticed. So did Bithia. The elder ghost murmured something soundless to her sister, but Cordelia didn't reply. Her gaze remained fixed on Eleanor's face.

The music played on. The children passed Buttercup back and forth, holding their own ceremony under the shadow of the thundercloud-filled day. Eleanor returned to her chair, book unopened, eyes distant.

Nan sat beside Mabel.

"Did you see that?" she whispered.

Mabel nodded. "Cordelia's looking at her like she looked at me when I wore white after Labor Day."

Nan stifled a snort.

Mabel softened. "But not mean. Not judging. Just... seeing. Like she recognizes something."

They watched the two women—one alive, one not—separated by time and breath but momentarily aligned.

The rain kept falling.

Inside, sugar melted on tongues, wings fluttered against china, and something ancient softened in the walls.

The house was full, after all.

Pickled Victory

Rain puddled on the courts in reflective patches, turning the whole of Pictona into a shimmering funhouse mirror. String lights drooped under the weight of the drizzle and ponchoed spectators huddled in makeshift shelters, sipping from foam cups of cocoa while their sneakers slowly soaked through. It was a scene both valiant and ridiculous—just as Mossy liked it.

He stood beneath the canopy with Rufus, both of them drenched, dripping, and entirely undeterred. Mossy had tied a towel around his neck like a sash of command. Rufus looked like he'd wandered out of a fishing documentary gone awry— helmet askew, paddle in hand, muttering about ligaments and destiny.

"We've been playing for hours," Rufus groaned, squishing his sock with a dramatic stomp. "Hours, Moss. I think my fingers are raisins."

"My dear fellow," Mossy said, brushing rain from his brow, "you are merely steeping in the brine of greatness. Like a fine dill."

Rufus gave him a look.

Mossy adjusted his whistle and blew it with flair. "Now

comes the final match. The clash of titans. The storm of destiny."

Rufus sighed. "Let me guess. The Shapiro Sisters?"

A whistle blew from across the court. Two figures emerged from the foggy sidelines like Valkyries in neon. Mildred and Gladys Shapiro wore matching thunderbolt-patterned compression sleeves and skorts so bright they could be seen from the stratosphere. Their gazes were weapons. Their paddles looked sharpened.

"I heard Mildred broke her last opponent's paddle with a single backhand," Rufus whispered.

"And Gladys's scowl educes watery bowels," Mossy said solemnly.

Rufus clutched his chest. "I don't think I'm emotionally prepared."

Mossy clapped him on the shoulder. "Neither was Odysseus, but he sailed anyway."

The match began with a crack of thunder that may or may not have been manufactured by Mildred's serve.

For the first ten minutes, it was chaos. Spectators gasped. Hot cocoa was spilled. Rufus slipped on a stray poncho and spun like a top. The ball ricocheted, bounced, whizzed.

Mossy shouted instructions between quotes from Homer and Horace. "Stand firm, noble pickle knight! Lo, yon dink doth approach!"

The Shapiro Sisters were merciless. Mildred's smashes came with battle cries. Gladys returned every shot with an expression of total disdain, as though the ball had offended her grandmother.

And yet somehow Mossy and Rufus held their ground.

Match point arrived with tension so thick it might have been meringue. Rain intensified, flattening hair and spirits alike. Rufus stood at the net, paddle trembling in his grip.

"This is it," Mossy murmured. "Spin it, soldier. Spin it like the earth depends on your wrist."

The ball came.

Mildred served. Rufus returned. Gladys lobbed. Mossy leapt, saving the point by sheer poetic willpower. Then Rufus, in a moment of divinely-inspired chaos, performed a spinning dink that would be spoken of for generations.

The ball danced.

Hovered.

Dropped.

Inside the line.

Cheers erupted.

Rufus collapsed onto the wet court, limbs splayed, paddle clutched to his chest like a war medal. "Victory!" he wheezed, then immediately winced and grabbed his lower back. "Ow. Nope. Something cracked. I think I broke my pride, and possibly my tailbone."

Gladys scowled. Mildred stomped. The Shapiro Sisters turned without a word and vanished into the drizzle, muttering about rigged whistles and suspicious spins.

The tournament official—an older man with heroic eyebrows and soaked socks—approached with two gold trophies and gold medals strung on damp ribbons. He draped one over Mossy's neck with the reverence of knighting a soggy poet.

Rufus didn't move. "Could someone just... toss mine gently in my general direction?" he asked from the ground.

Mossy leaned over. "You all right, old friend?"

"I made the wish," Rufus groaned. "Right there in your study, remember? I wished we'd win. I should've been more specific about not injuring my backside in the process."

Mossy's eyes widened slightly. "The paw."

Rufus gave a pained nod. "Cursed wish confirmed. It granted me victory and whacked me square on the dignity."

Mossy helped him upright, careful of the grimace on Rufus's face as he hobbled to his feet. A bystander handed him the second medal with a sympathetic wince.

Once steady enough to hold the mic, Mossy cleared his throat and declared:

"Ladies, gentlemen, and fellow connoisseurs of court-bound glory, today we have seen that true bravery is not measured in dry socks or unbruised tailbones. No. It is found in the slosh of shoes, the flick of wrists, and the noble refusal to yield to thunder or neon skorts. We, like Sir Percy Fawcett of old, sought the mythic. And in the fog of battle, we found it. We found... victory."

A murmur of applause rose from the cocoa-stained crowd. Someone shouted, "That man deserves a statue!"

Rufus raised a trembling hand and winced.

They walked home like rain-drenched war heroes, hefty trophies clutched in their hands. Flooded roads had turned to shallow rivers, and at one intersection they ran across the couple floating in the canoe, beers still in hand.

"You guys win?" they called.

"Indeed," Mossy replied, raising his medal. "The skorts have been conquered. But at great personal cost."

And somewhere, behind a shuttered window, a monkey paw gave the tiniest twitch.

Schemes and Scribbles

∿

Rain drummed a steady rhythm against the windows, wrapping the old house in a lullaby of gray light and mist. But inside the parlor it was anything but sleepy.

The fireplace crackled with soft insistence, its glow warming the green-tiled hearth and casting flickers over the old bookshelves and damask curtains. The scent of cinnamon, clove, and lemony polish mingled in the air—punctuated now and then by the buttery echo of something sweet lingering from the last round of scones.

Bea skipped across the Persian rug, her red galoshes thumping with each joyous step. Arms outstretched, sleeves flapping like wings, she spun and shouted, "I'm a wish for wings!"

Ollie stood nearby in full detective mode—hands clamped into robot claws, eyes narrowed with intent. He moved in jerky, mechanical bursts. "Robot dog activated," he intoned. "Would you like tea or a tail wag?"

Nan sat cross-legged near the lace-draped tea trolley, beside a tin of cookies and a crayon-streaked pile of paper. The parlor's low lighting pooled around her like honey. She clapped. "Marvelous drawings, children. I believe that one was 'pixie sleeps in teacups'."

Ollie grinned and held up his notepad, full of wildly imaginative traps. There were springboards and pulley systems; one looked suspiciously like it launched netting from a whisk. "That one uses your rolling pin, by the way."

Nan peered at it closely. "It's quite... inventive. You ought to consider a career in engineering."

"Thanks," he said with a cheerful tone. "I'm determined to catch that monkey paw. It's definitely granting wishes. I heard you wish for the house to be full of guests, and then it started raining, bringing everyone here. Now I want to make my own wish."

Nan smiled.

Ollie continued, "But I still need the ideal bait. Maybe a banana will do."

Over by the hearth, the mahjong table had taken over the rug. Mabel, Eleanor, Susan, and Tom—and the ever-colorful Kiki and Brent—were mid-round, teacups abandoned in favor of full concentration.

Mabel slapped down a tile. "Well, butter my begonias and toss me in the compost! That was my tile!"

Eleanor chuckled, cheeks pink with real amusement. Susan grinned behind her mug. Even Kiki cracked a smile, nudging her fiancé. "I swear this place gets weirder by the hour."

Brent shrugged as he dealt tiles. "That's what the reviews said."

"We aim to please," Nan called over her shoulder, ferrying a fresh tray of tea.

Passing with the teapot, she smiled at Bea. "What do you have there, sugarplum?"

Bea kept her gaze steady. "This is my treasure map. The dragons stand watch over the ladders, and the flowers mark the locations of the fairy houses." Nan leaned closer, her heart melting like warm shortbread.

"In that case," she murmured, "you should protect it as if it's your most cherished secret."

Mabel swept the winning line with the triumph of a general. "Snapdragon strike!"

"Does she always swear with flower names?" Brent asked.

Eleanor leaned in conspiratorially. "It seems she does. And she means every petal."

Nan handed her guest a fresh cup of chamomile. Eleanor's fingers wrapped around it tightly.

"Thank you," she said.

Nan caught her eye. There was a softness there now, a loosening.

Across the parlor, Ollie had returned to his planning. This time, they used napkin rings as wheels and attempted to rig a trap using embroidery floss and two upside-down teacups.

"That's not structurally sound," Ollie muttered, adjusting the string.

Bea jumped off her dad's lap and plopped next to Ollie while pointing toward the bookshelf. "I wish we had a pulley. Or a unicorn."

Nan smiled. She bent beside them and whispered, "Do you know what the best trap is?"

Both children leaned in.

Before Nan could respond, a distinct *skitter-skitter* sound scurried through the room. The monkey paw streaked beneath the tea trolley.

Ollie's eyes widened. "There it is!"

He took off like a shot. Bea followed. They darted between the legs of chairs, across the Persian rug, and—

CRASH.

Tiles went flying. Mabel let out a strangled, "Oh, dandelion down!"

Eleanor burst into laughter. It started small, a little puff of air, and then bloomed into something real and full. Susan had to set down her cup to dab her eyes.

"Pixies, pudding, and pawprints," Mabel muttered, brushing crumbs from her blouse.

Eleanor was still giggling, her eyes brighter than Nan had yet seen.

From the other side of the room, Ollie returned with his notepad. It now had three new diagrams and a wish list written in pencil.

(Ollie's List of Wishes)

A robot dog that barks

Teleportation (but only for fun, not emergencies)

Endless dessert

The ability to speak to cats

For Eleanor to smile every day

Nan pretended not to notice the last one, but her throat tightened anyway.

She folded the paper and tucked it into her apron. "Every great inventor starts with a napkin drawing."

Just then, Thistle peeked out from a sugar bowl, sugar dust coating his hair like frost. He blinked sleepily and gave her a thumbs-up before vanishing again.

The Hero Returns

Thunder cracked overhead like a celestial timpani as the front door flew open. Rain misted in behind a pair of soggy silhouettes framed by lightning.

Mossy stepped through the threshold with theatrical flair, arms raised in triumph. His soaked fishing waders squelched with every step, and his shirt clung to him like a deflated sail. A shiny medal swung from a red ribbon around his neck.

"Ladies and gentlemen," he boomed, voice reverberating against the parlor walls, "victory is ours!"

Rufus followed close behind, his helmet askew, his poncho clinging to him like wet tissue paper. He pointed proudly to the matching medal at his throat. "I won, too," he announced, then winced as he gingerly shifted his weight. "Mostly. Except for my tailbone. I think I cracked it doing that winning dink."

Nan's brows rose. "You what?"

"He landed like a sack of wet laundry," Mossy offered helpfully. "But oh, it was glorious."

Behind them, the Shapiro Sisters entered like twin storm clouds. Mildred's skort was damp to the knees and her expression could curdle cream. Gladys gave a tight nod and muttered something about faulty court conditions and questionable footwear.

Together, the four of them squelched across the floor, leaving wet footprints and the scent of brine in their wake. Rufus hobbled with exaggerated care, clutching the small of his back like a man twice his age.

Mabel emerged from the parlor with a hand to her heart. "What on earth happened to you all?"

"Greatness happened," Mossy declared. "Against thunder and tide, wind and wail, Rufus and I triumphed in the championship match."

"And then I was betrayed by gravity," Rufus muttered. "My spine is suing for damages."

Mabel smiled. "Did you beat the skort squad or just tire them out?"

Gladys sniffed. Mildred crossed her arms. "They got lucky."

Rufus beamed through the pain. "We got scrappy. And I landed the winning dink."

He mimed his final shot with an exaggerated flourish, only to flinch halfway through and clutch his rear. A few guests applauded anyway.

Mossy bowed with a puddle-sloshing flourish, then turned to Nan with gallant purpose. Dropping to one knee—rain-drizzled and beaming—he held up the small gold trophy as if it were Excalibur itself.

"My love," he said solemnly, "in the grand tradition of knights returning from valiant quest, I offer you this most cherished treasure. Spray-painted, perhaps. Plastic, undoubtedly. But won in your honor, and with every drop of soggy courage I possess."

Nan, cheeks pinking, took the trophy with a gracious

curtsy and a spark in her eye. "Then it shall hold pride of place on the parlor mantel."

Mossy rose and leaned in with a roguish whisper meant only for her. "Perhaps tonight, milady, I'll present you with a few verses of victory in private."

"I look forward to it, Mossy darling."

Gladys ran her hands over her damp skort with a grimace. "I swear this thing shrank three sizes. I'm going to need a shoehorn to get it off."

Mildred crossed her arms, eyeing Rufus with mock suspicion. "That spin-dink was lucky."

Rufus puffed out his chest. "That spin-dink was artistry. You saw it."

Gladys snorted. "We saw flailing and divine intervention."

Rufus grinned, then winced again as he tried to straighten. "Next time, I'm bringing a cape and a cushion."

Nan stepped in, hands on her hips and eyes twinkling. "All right, you four champions of the puddle realm—towels are in the hallway linen chest, second drawer. Dry yourselves before you flood the parquet. Dinner will be served in the formal dining room in exactly twenty minutes. No dripping allowed."

"And where might one find a donut pillow?" Rufus asked, still hunched.

"I'll get the memory foam one," Mabel said, already heading toward the linen closet. "And a bag of ice."

As she disappeared down the hall, a glint of gold caught the light from the mantel.

Several pixies fluttered down from the rafters—Thistle with his tufted hair standing straight up from static, and Tansy still trailing droplets from her lavender wings. They hovered above the trophy like archaeologists discovering a relic.

Neat poked it with a sugar-crusted finger.

Bitter perched on the little gold paddle and mimed a victorious cheer, wings flaring with delight.

Bea gasped. "They're inspecting it!"

Ollie, eyes wide, whispered, "They know it's cursed."

"It's not cursed, dear boy," Mossy said, overhearing as he shook rain from his sleeves. "It's legendary. A testament to strategy, perseverance, and superior dink formation."

He turned to Nan, then to the gathering guests. "I propose we open a proper bottle of Champagne to celebrate the glorious rise of the Paddle Paladins!"

Rufus blinked. "That's us?"

"That's us," Mossy confirmed. "Long may we reign, provided my partner doesn't throw out the rest of his spine."

Rufus gave a thumbs-up from his hunched position. "Still mostly intact."

Nan sighed, affectionate and exasperated all at once. "The formal dining room. Twenty minutes. And no pixie duels on the chandelier this time."

The Banquet of Bewilderments

The dining room at the Nettles B&B glowed like something conjured from a forgotten fairytale. A long damask-draped table stretched through the room like a river of ivory and gold. Silver vases stood sentry down the center—polished to a near-mirror shine—each overflowing with ruby-hued roses, their velvet petals matching the teacups set precisely beside each plate. The pattern danced across the Royal Albert china like a remembered melody: red blooms, curling stems, scalloped edges kissed with gold.

Candlelight flickered in vintage sconces and from the tall tapers nestled among pumpkins, mums, and cinnamon sticks. The light shimmered across crystal glassware, catching the facets like diamonds; broken rainbows flickering on napkins and forearms. And beneath it all, a delicate hum from the gramophone as *Carmen* spilled into the air, each rising note twining through the steam of roasted rosemary and red wine sauce.

Nan swept in with the first course like a queen bearing offerings. Her white apron crisply ironed, her pearls catching the firelight at her wrist as she lowered the tureen. Beneath the apron, her silk blouse glowed soft pink—something blush and ladylike—and her heels clicked gently as she moved.

Behind her, Mabel's entrance was all drama and delight. Her apron, embroidered with a rose and tabby cat, flared as she spun with a tray of pumpkin bisque cups. Her lipstick was as bold as her stride, and her laugh—a low, rich chuckle—carried across the table.

A cloud of pixies darted behind them like miniature waitstaff in training. Tansy mimed a cork pop with a fizz of gold light bursting from her fingertips, while Bitter hovered over the breadbasket, sprinkling crumbs like a blessing. No one at the table seemed to notice them besides Bea and Ollie, who ducked to avoid a glittery loop-the-loop.

Nan placed the bisque at each setting, hands steady and warm. "Tonight is our modest meal," she said, voice pitched to cut through the music and murmur. "Tomorrow, of course, is the grand Thanksgiving feast—three p.m. sharp. Continental breakfast will be laid out in the sunroom at eight."

Mabel leaned in, grinning. "And anyone wearing a hat gets bonus pie."

Nan shot her a dry look. "Mabel."

Mabel fluttered her lashes. "Don't discourage accessories."

The clink of silverware resumed. Guests tucked napkins into laps. Somewhere under the table, a pixie let out a tiny hiccup.

At the far end, Rufus eased into his seat with a theatrical groan. The donut pillow beneath him gave a pathetic squish.

"Cursed coccyx," he muttered. "Feels like I got rear-ended by karma."

Mossy passed him a glass of cider. "Poetic justice has a particular aim, dear boy."

Rufus squinted. "You think it was the monkey paw? Because I swear, I sat on it, wished to win, and now I can barely bend."

The Shapiro Sisters, seated across from him in matching shawls and bristling indignation, exchanged sharp glances.

Mildred leaned forward, pointing her fork like a fencing foil. "I *knew* black magic was in play. I felt it in my serve."

Gladys huffed beside her, her scarf tied like a bandana. "You don't just accidentally dink like that. It was unnatural. Your form was suspiciously fluid."

Rufus gave a beleaguered shrug. "My form is a mystery even to me."

Kiki looked up from her camera. "You guys are blaming sorcery for losing a pickleball game?"

Brent finally spoke. "Imagination gets real lively during a downpour. And yet, we did see something stutter about."

Murmurs stirred through the room like cinnamon in cider.

Mossy, seated near the fireplace with his medal still gleaming from his pocket, raised his glass. "If poetry can turn a storm into a sonnet, I daresay magic can meddle in sports. We dined on destiny and drank from the chalice of chance. If a monkey paw made it so, then we raise our glasses to fate's absurdity."

"Speak for your coccyx," Rufus muttered, wincing.

Across the table Eleanor sipped quietly, her expression unreadable but not uninterested. The firelight carved soft shadows across her cheekbones, and her gaze lingered not on the duck or the roses but on the flickering candle flame reflected in her wine.

Kiki, glamorously slouched in a slinky red dress, held her phone at chest height, angling it for the perfect shot. "Say it again," she whispered to her fiancé. "Call this plate *hauntingly delicious.*"

He blinked. "It's a salad."

"That's why it's ironic."

Nan passed behind her with a tray of rolls, one brow arched.

Bea's giggle rang out as she poked her fork into a sugared walnut. Her brother reached for the breadbasket with detective-like stealth.

The moment held—shimmering like the light on the glasses, like the laughter hovering just beneath conversation. Then Mossy stood, one hand on his heart.

"My friends," he said grandly, "may this night be remembered as the eve of bounty. A feast not just of duck and bisque but of company, curiosity, and the occasional need for a good cushion."

A ripple of applause. Eleanor's lips quirked upward.

As dessert plates were cleared and the wine flowed more freely, the conversation turned speculative, sparking like kindling in a dry hearth.

"If the monkey paw's powers were real," Brent said with a smirk, "what would you even wish for?"

"Teleportation," Ollie said immediately, sitting up so straight his fork clattered to the floor. "Or a swimming pool full of pudding. No—flying. No—time travel. Wait. Can I wish for multiple wishes?"

"Perhaps if the paw's in a generous mood," Mabel said, her voice dry as one of the cinnamon sticks nestled in the garland.

Kiki leaned forward, resting her chin in one manicured hand. "#MonkeyPawManifesting," she murmured. "Do I wish for followers? Better lighting in my food shots? A contract with that new app?" She sipped from her Champagne flute. "No—penthouse in Paris. View of the Eiffel Tower. And a walk-in closet with a rotating shoe wall."

Brent raised his glass. "Flat in Manhattan. A Ferrari. In red."

Kiki's eyes sparkled. "To match my heels. The content we'd get."

Mossy swirled his cider. "So many extravagant wishes. You know what I'd ask for?"

Rufus groaned, shifting carefully on his donut pillow. "I would wish for a new tailbone."

Mossy smiled wistfully. "A single stanza of unpublished Keats. Or maybe Poe's missing pages. Something lost to time."

"Always poetry," Nan said fondly.

"I sneezed and saw stars," Rufus muttered. "My coccyx has cursed me with cosmic insight."

Across the table, Eleanor set down her wine. "I'd rather not wish for anything," she said softly. "Not anymore."

A pause.

Cordelia and Bithia floated silently into the archway, their translucent forms just visible to those attuned to oddities. Bithia's gown shimmered like moth wings; Cordelia looked particularly solid tonight, her chignon pinned with Victorian severity.

Cordelia sniffed. "Wishing never ends well. Not with that thing."

"I thought you both were upstairs," Mabel whispered.

"Dearest, we go where we are needed. You should know that by now," Bithia replied with a wistful air.

Cordelia blew out one of the candle tapers with a sharp puff of spectral air. The flame sputtered and died, plunging half the table into a flickering chiaroscuro.

Bea gasped. Ollie scribbled "ghost intervention" into his notebook with frantic glee.

"All right, let's settle this once and for all," Nan said, rising with a cloche in hand. "If the monkey paw is still in this house—"

But before she could finish, a scratching sound emanated from the table like leprechauns tapdancing.

The monkey paw launched from the centerpiece, its

leathery fingers knocking over a wine glass. Red liquid sloshed across the damask in an elegant horror show.

"IT'S REAL!" Tom shouted, leaping up with his napkin held like a dueling glove.

Susan shrieked and ducked behind the floral arrangement. Rufus tried to stand quickly and winced mid-rise, muttering.

The Shapiro Sisters sprang into coordinated action. Mildred swung her empty wine goblet. Gladys wielded a salad fork like a dagger.

"I knew black magic was in play!" Mildred cried. "That dink wasn't natural!"

Kiki shrieked and whipped out her phone. "#Demonic-DinnerParty!"

Nan tried to trap the paw beneath the silver cloche, but it was faster—skittering across the table, flipping a bread roll, tangling itself briefly in the table runner before bounding off again.

A flicker of gold light indicated the pixies were in pursuit, brandishing serving forks and butter knives like knights of the petit four.

Bea squealed with glee and dove after it. Ollie followed, his notebook clutched in one hand, a dinner roll in the other.

"Be careful, darlings!" Nan called after them.

The monkey paw zipped toward the staircase, the children on its heels, a pixie riding it like a whisky-crazed cowboy.

And just like that, it was gone.

Silence dropped like a velvet curtain.

A chair sat crooked. The candle still guttered. Rufus gingerly eased back onto his donut cushion with a whimper.

Nan set the cloche down with an exhale. "That's the last time we serve four courses with a cursed centerpiece."

Mabel, rising with her dignity mostly intact, sighed. "Next time, we go buffet-style."

Cordelia muttered, "And scented candles. Sandalwood masks mischief."

Bithia nodded sagely. "Or apricot."

Eleanor lifted her teacup again, but this time a small smile curled at the edges.

And high above, on the second-floor landing, a faint glow traced the hallway shadows—just the flicker of pixie wings and the soft pitter-patter of wish-laced chaos.

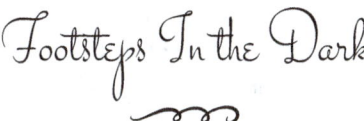

Footsteps In the Dark

The house had hushed.

It was the kind of silence that came only after laughter had emptied out, after clinking glasses had gone still, after every good story had been told—twice. Candle stubs flickered low in their holders, puddling wax into silver trays. Somewhere in the distance the gramophone let out a soft, contented hum of static, like a sigh too tired to become music.

Mossy leaned against the dining room doorframe, the last button of his collar undone and his tie draped rakishly over one shoulder. He watched Nan in the candlelight, polishing the final streak from the long table like a priestess closing up after some sacred rite.

"Darling," he murmured, his voice low and reverent, "this evening was a triumph. Fit for queens, poets, and conquering athletes with compromised tailbones."

Nan didn't look up. "Don't flirt with me while I'm brandishing lemon oil."

"But it smells like citrus redemption in here," he countered, stepping fully into the room. His loafers made no sound against the parquet.

Nan gave the silver tray one last swipe, straightened the center-piece roses, and finally turned to face him. Her cheeks still held the warmth of wine and candlelight. "I could sleep for a week."

"You may," he said gallantly, "but not until I sing you a sonnet and pour you something scandalous."

She rolled her eyes, but there was fondness in the gesture. "You'd flirt with a coat rack if it had good bone structure."

"I *have* done," Mossy replied, deadpan. "There was that one in Vienna."

"You're impossible."

"I'm devoted."

"You're still standing here instead of fetching our nightcap."

He lifted his hands in surrender. "At your command, mi reina. But the question remains—what's the mood for our nightcap? Elegant absinthe? Rowdy mezcal? The one that tastes like the ghost of a smoked pinecone?"

Nan peeled off her apron and folded it precisely. "The white bottle with the blue flowers."

Mossy placed a hand over his heart. "Clase Azul. A double, I assume?"

"Triple if you're pouring slowly."

He chuckled, already stepping toward the sideboard where the spirits lived in cheerful defiance of bedtime. "A bold request. Are you planning to seduce me?"

She turned at the threshold of the room, one hand on the doorframe, her pearls catching the dying light like fireflies. "Depends how fast you pour."

Then she was gone—through the back yard to the Mossy Mobile, their cozy abode for the evening. There she would immerse herself in her evening rituals: tonics and terrycloth and, presumably, the small brush for her eyebrows she treated like a sacred relic.

Mossy exhaled a soft laugh, one hand resting on the bottle. He didn't pour just yet. The house had grown still again in her absence, and he found he rather liked it.

It was rare, this quiet—the kind that felt like listening in on something ancient. Rain tapped faintly at the windows. Somewhere, a pipe in the wall gave a polite burble. The scent of lemon oil lingered in the air, mixed with rosemary, clove, and the ghost of wine sauce. It smelled not of food but of *after*: after joy, after effort, after magic.

He walked the length of the table, fingers trailing the carved edge, admiring the silver's softened gleam. It had been a beautiful dinner.

No—he corrected himself. *She* had made it beautiful.

He turned toward the hearth and the flickering shadows, his voice low as if speaking to the walls. "A modest supper, she said. Modest, like Versailles was a modest cottage."

There was a creak behind him. Not floorboards. Not footsteps, exactly. Something subtler.

Mossy glanced toward the dark archway.

"Ah," he said, not startled, just amused. "Late-night haunting, is it?"

A soft swirl of air passed his shoulder, cooler than the lemon-scented warmth that still clung to the room. In the corner near the grandfather clock, a shimmer of shape began to take form. Gossamer outlines. A faint Victorian hemline. A ringlet hovering in the air before settling into view.

Cordelia. Her silhouette was crisp tonight—starched, in fact. As if the candlelight had drawn her out of memory and into form.

A moment later, Bithia appeared beside her like ink blooming in water—graceful, gentle, already tilting her head at Mossy with a bemused smile.

"Did you enjoy this evening's dinner?" he asked, grasping

the bottle from the sideboard now, uncorking it with a practiced twist.

"You made quite a speech," Bithia murmured, her voice barely disturbing the air. "It seemed rude to interrupt."

Cordelia floated closer to the roses, her expression unreadable. "The duck was overcooked."

"You're incorporeal," Mossy said, pouring two fingers' worth into his glass. "What do you know about duck?"

Cordelia didn't blink. "Standards transcend death."

Mossy took a slow sip and leaned against the chair Nan had just polished. "Do spirits make wishes?"

The question hung for a beat, suspended like dust in candlelight.

"No," Bithia said. "That's the province of the living."

Mossy swirled the golden liquid in his glass. "That's a shame. Life without wishing would be frightfully dull."

Cordelia gave a faint, imperious sniff. "Wishing is childish."

Mossy smiled. "So is poetry. And yet both have endured."

Bithia tilted her head, and her voice softened further. "What would *you* wish for, sir?"

Mossy glanced at the back door through which Nan had exited, the delicate fragrance of her rose lotion still in the air.

He didn't answer at once.

Instead he looked down into his glass, then raised it slowly. "To hold on to every golden hour. And to know when I'm in one."

There was a long silence. Even Cordelia didn't scoff.

Then Mossy offered the ghosts a wry smile. "Well. You float through your evening hour, I'll sip through mine. Cheers."

He raised the glass, and Bithia nodded with a wistful smile. Cordelia rolled her eyes so hard it may have shifted the curtains.

And from somewhere upstairs the distant creak of a door settling echoed down the hall, as if the house itself sighed: *Yes. The day is done. Almost.*

Nightcaps and Knowing Cooks

The warm glow of the lamp in the Mossy Mobile bathed the bed in amber light, illuminating the hand-sewn quilt and the heap of pillows. Nan leisurely combed her hair, the soothing aroma of her lavender night oil wafting gently like a lullaby. From the tiny en suite bathroom came the sound of running water, a few off-tune notes of a sea shanty, and the familiar thud of Mossy accidentally toppling the soap dish once more.

She smiled to herself, placing the brush aside. The estate had embraced its night rhythm—frogs croaked by the pond, the sea breeze sighed, and the occasional giggle from the pixies under the eaves fluttered down like leaves on wind.

The bathroom door swung all the way open as Mossy entered the main cabin, robes loose and glasses fogged. He extended his hand towards the two tumblers resting on the small table beside the tall white and blue bottle of Clase Azul Reposado tequila.

"For you, my enchantress," he said, bowing low as he handed her the glass. "A potion most divine. Notes of vanilla and spice. And possibly wizardry."

Nan accepted it with a raised brow. "You did go for the triple pour. Are you planning to seduce me, Mossy darling?"

"Madam," he intoned solemnly, clinking his glass to hers. "I live in perpetual hope."

They sipped, letting the rich warmth settle between them. Mossy sat on the edge of the bed, shrugging off his robe to reveal a T-shirt with a faded print of Byron wearing sunglasses. Nan joined him, curling one leg beneath her as she took the glass from his hand and set both drinks on the nightstand.

With practiced ease she reached behind him, thumbs pressing into the tight knots near his shoulder blades.

He groaned, melting forward. "You were born with hands blessed by angels."

"You just carry all your stress in your back."

"I appreciate your method. The relief is immediate," he sighed.

They moved in quiet rhythm, the hush between them filled only by the ticking of the little porcelain clock on the side table. They had done this thousands of times—the shoulder rub, the shared drink, the warmth of touch that needed no permission. A ritual carved into the grain of their days. No matter where they lay their head at night.

Nan let her hands rest on his back for a long moment. Then:

"I was thinking about the paw," she said softly.

Mossy tilted his head just enough to signal listening.

"It didn't just fall out of that trunk. None of them ever do. The music box." She paused, touching the key that dangled from the chain about her neck. "They appear when... well, when someone needs them."

He straightened slightly, nodding. "When someone can break the curse. Or carry the weight."

"Or both," she whispered.

She moved to snuggle in closer, their shoulders brushing. Her tone was thoughtful, not fearful.

"Do you think it's the house doing it? Releasing the items? Not Bithia?"

Mossy looked out the small window, toward the house where the old floorboards creaked and the attic held secrets from the past.

"Oh, you thought it was Bithia." He rubbed his chin. "I hadn't considered." He thought for a few long moments. "Indeed," he said. "I do think it's most likely the house."

Nan clapped her hands together, "As if it's... listening. And remembering."

He gestured vaguely upward. "Like it holds on to those objects until just the right moment. Until someone arrives who's knotted up just so. Someone with a bruise on their heart in the exact shape the object understands."

Nan rested her head on his shoulder. "It feels like matchmaking."

"Between grief and grace," Mossy agreed.

Nan was quiet for a long time.

"Then who is the paw for?" she asked at last.

Mossy didn't answer right away. His fingers played with the edge of the quilt.

"I'm not sure," he said finally. "Maybe Eleanor. Maybe Ollie. Maybe Mabel, though heaven help us if it grants her a flower that blooms through concrete. Maybe it hasn't finished choosing."

Nan sighed. "I detest not knowing."

"I love not knowing," Mossy replied, smiling at the ceiling. "It means the story still has pages left."

She kissed his shoulder. "You're such a romantic."

"I live with you. It rubs off."

Another long silence passed, gentle and easy.

Nan reached for his hand. "I already have everything I ever wished for."

Mossy turned to her, gaze soft and adoring. "Oh, I can still think of one thing."

He kissed her then, a slow, familiar warmth that tasted of honey and lemon.

She giggled as she pulled back. "The lamp, Mossy dear."

He reached to click it off.

The frogs creaked on.

Somewhere in the house, the monkey paw skittered once across the kitchen floor.

No one heard it.

Only the house did.

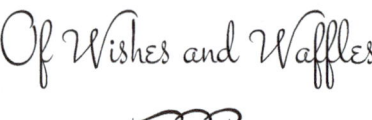

Of Wishes and Waffles

Rain smudged the windows in lazy vertical lines, soft and silver as pencil shavings. The storm still grumbled overhead, but inside was all warmth and breakfast-laced bliss.

Mossy settled into his favorite wingback in the corner of the parlor, the newspaper a loose accordion on his lap. His slippers were comfy, his teacup half-full, and the last of the waffle syrup clung sweetly to his lower lip. Across the room a fire burbled in the hearth, coaxing a gentle steam from damp socks and velvet robes.

He glanced over the top of his bifocals and watched the morning unfold.

Bea and Ollie were belly-flat on the floral rug, heads propped on elbows, eyes glued to the television. The Macy's Thanksgiving Day Parade shimmered across the screen, all oversized balloons and clunky choreography. When the Sesame Street float appeared Bea let out a delighted squeal, drumming her feet against the floor.

"Elmo!"

Ollie, however, was all business. He adjusted his safety goggles and returned to the odd contraption spread out beside him: a mousetrap connected to a spoon catapult, a paper cup rigged with string, and a suspiciously glittery banana in the center.

"You think this'll work?" Bea whispered, eyes wide.

"It's based on leverage and pixie distraction," Ollie replied solemnly. "The banana is irresistible. Probably."

Mossy chuckled into his tea. "Engineering and enchantment, the twin pillars of boyhood."

Across the parlor, Nan and Mabel flitted in and out of the dining room like hummingbirds in house slippers. They were clearing the remnants of breakfast—stacked china plates kissed with cranberry compote, empty tea pots that had long since cooled, platters bearing only crumbs. Each trip was performed with the flurry and flourish of a dance.

To Mossy, they were nothing less than kitchen sprites mid-ballet. If he squinted, he could almost hear Rimsky-Korsakov's "Flight of the Bumblebee" chasing them down the hallway.

The buffet had been a morning poem of its own: golden waffles with warm maple syrup, pumpkin scones dotted with cranberries, buttery scrambled eggs beside baked apples glazed in cinnamon. There had been fruit platters shaped like harvest cornucopias, and coffee strong enough to resurrect the sleepiest of men.

Most of the guests still lounged in pajamas or robes, nestled on tufted chairs with slippers dangling off toes. The parlor hummed with easy conversation and clinking spoons. Outside, the thunder muttered without commitment.

From above the mantel pixies hovered lazily, mirroring the floats on television. Thistle twirled like a baton, his wings catching firelight, while Tansy performed synchronized flips whenever a new balloon appeared.

Of all the guests, only Ollie and Bea could see the pixie performance. That much was clear. The two children shared whispered giggles and sidelong glances, especially when Brash pretended to deflate like a saggy Snoopy.

"Gotcha!"

The snap of the mousetrap sent every adult jolting. The catapult spoon launched. A metal mixing bowl slammed down. Pixie glitter exploded into the air like confetti.

Nan poked her head in from the hallway, teacup in hand. "What on earth was that?"

Ollie grinned like a magician revealing a final trick. "Captured!"

He knelt beside the contraption and slowly lifted the bowl. Beneath it, squirming slightly and clicking one mummified claw, was the monkey paw.

A hush fell over the room.

Guests leaned forward. Mabel dropped a teacup into the sink with a clatter. The fire crackled.

Ollie fished a folded paper from his pocket. "My wish list," he declared.

Cordelia and Bithia silently floated in through the far wall, nearly unnoticed, their ethereal forms framed in morning light. Cordelia looked mildly alarmed. Bithia looked curious.

Ollie began reading.

"Number one: a robot dog that brings snacks. Number two: teleportation. Number three: a swimming pool full of chocolate pudding—but only if it's the good kind."

Bea giggled into her hands. Brent raised a brow. Kiki filmed.

Ollie paused.

His gaze moved to Eleanor, seated quietly near the fire, hands wrapped around her tea.

He looked back at the list. Then down at the bowl trapping the paw.

With deliberate reverence and tactical nimbleness he

reached out and snatched the paw, raising it high above his head.

"I wish Eleanor's daughter wakes up and they live happily ever after."

Time held its breath.

The monkey paw shimmered, faintly at first—then gold light pulsed through each withered finger. It glowed brighter, curling in slowly until it formed a closed fist. The glow receded.

It lay still.

The storm outside broke. Raindrops faded into mist. The wind hushed. Light filtered through the clouds like a sigh.

Rufus grabbed at his tushie, a slight grin on his face.

Cordelia whispered, "Such boldness from someone so small."

Bithia added, "It is not the hand but the heart that defines a wish."

Ollie sat back on his heels.

The room exhaled.

Then Eleanor's phone rang.

She stared at it. Her hands trembled. Everyone waited.

She answered. "Hello?"

A pause.

Then: "She's awake?" Her voice was barely audible. "She's... really awake? Talking? No, don't move her yet. Just... oh. Oh."

Tears streaked down her cheeks.

Bea squealed with joy. Mabel dropped a plate and clapped. The pixies exploded into air spirals. Even Cordelia smiled before dissolving into the wallpaper.

Kiki, already holding her phone at a cinematic angle, whispered, "We are *so* live." Then louder, with practiced breathlessness:

"Miracle on Thanksgiving! A magical stay at the most

enchanted B&B in Florida—y'all, I am crying. #Gratitude-Glow #MagicIsReal #EnchantedStay #B&BBliss #ThankfulTears"!

Her fiancé leaned in from behind, dabbing his eyes with a napkin. "And the waffles were amazing."

Mossy knelt beside Ollie.

"My boy," he said softly, "dreams are the kindling of wonder. But to give your wish away—that is alchemy. May you always be a fountain of wishes."

Ollie flushed bright pink. "I didn't need the pudding one."

Mossy stood, brushing his knees. "Well, then! I believe the spell is broken, the storm has passed, and if I'm not mistaken the lady of the house will now wish to reclaim her parlor."

Nan swept in like a general with a tablecloth. "Thirty minutes, people. That turkey is not going to garnish itself. Formal attire encouraged. Pixies, into your dinner jackets."

Mabel added with a wink, "Bonus pie for anyone wearing sparkles."

Kiki looked up. "I have rhinestone heels."

Brent sighed. "Of course you do."

The guests began to stir, their excitement mounting. The mood had shifted entirely, from sleepy contentment to something bright. Buoyant. Blessed.

The monkey paw, now curled like a spent seed pod, rested gently in Ollie's back pocket.

The spell had been lifted.

And somewhere, unseen by the rest, Bithia touched the parlor wall and whispered, "How marvelous."

The house, as always, listened.

Feast Of the Unexpected

The Thanksgiving table was a quiet masterpiece, the kind that didn't shout for attention but glowed with warmth in every detail. The Spode Woodland china glinted with elegant nostalgia, each plate a rustic canvas of leaping stags and wild turkeys. Pumpkins, hollowed and filled with golden mums, formed the heart of the centerpiece, flanked by taper candles in brass holders that flickered gently.

The room itself hummed with a reverent hush, broken only by the occasional clink of silver or the low hum of a vintage record spinning something soft and orchestral in the background. Pixies, having worn themselves out in the earlier chaos, slumbered in little gourds tucked into the garland, their glow barely perceptible—like embers, dreaming.

Nan had changed from her apron into a deep-wine-colored satin dress, her lipstick a perfect match, her pearl earrings catching the light as she moved. Mossy, freshly shaven and dashing, wore a dark green velvet jacket with a silk pocket square folded just so.

Mabel swept in, arms dramatically outstretched to display

her hat, which brimmed with chrysanthemums. "Behold! The spirit of autumn in headwear!"

"Looks like the spirit of autumn ran headfirst into a florist," Rufus muttered from the far end of the table, adjusting the oversized pilgrim hat balanced precariously on his head.

Guests had arrived in everything from cozy knits to vintage suits. Kiki wore a champagne-colored cocktail dress with crystals scattered like dewdrops. Brent had managed a blazer over his graphic tee. Eleanor, serene as moonlight, wore a subdued navy twill set with a vintage pin and her hair pulled up in a twist. The smile in her eyes made her look years younger.

They gathered around the table like a mismatched collection of ornaments—different shapes and stories, none of them blood-related yet somehow threaded together.

Mabel wielded the carving knife like a stage prop.

Rufus blinked. "That might be the most threatening thing I've seen all day."

Mabel winked and sliced with theatrical precision. The turkey yielded under her knife with a triumphant sigh, releasing a savory perfume as steam curled upward, laced with thyme, rosemary, and a hint of orange zest. The scent seemed to soften everyone's shoulders at once.

Dishes began to pass from hand to hand like sacred offerings. Golden cornbread stuffing laced with fresh sage, cranberry chutney glistening like rubies under candlelight. Nearby, a tiered tray held cranberry-Brie crescent bites, each one topped with a sprig of rosemary and a single candied pecan—fragrant, gooey, and glowing.

Nan proudly displayed a plate of harvest chicken skewers, their caramelized glaze catching the flicker of the tapers. Kumquat marmalade shimmered in tiny jars like captured sunsets, nestled next to individual bowls of pumpkin soup so velvety it could have passed for a dream. Its aroma drifted warmly through the air—nutmeg, cream, and something softly roasted.

A wide bowl of autumn harvest salad—crisp apples, toasted pecans, jewel-like pomegranate seeds, and crumbles of blue cheese—gleamed under a drizzle of cider vinaigrette. The tang balanced the sweetness of nearby scones: pumpkin, flaky and warm, topped with cinnamon-spice whipped cream that clung like a first snowfall.

Mossy rose slightly, one hand on the back of Nan's chair, raising his glass with the other.

"To strange storms," he began, voice warm and round as the goblets of wine, "unexpected guests, and the quiet power of kindness. May the road always rise to meet us—and may we never underestimate a rainy-day wish."

The clink of crystal was gentle and sincere, a murmur of assent passing around the table like a shared breath.

Brent raised his glass with a wicked grin and gently clinked it against Kiki's, whispering something in her ear that caused her to blush.

Eleanor, seated beside Ollie, set down her fork and took a second slice of pie with unexpected gusto. The moment hovered soft and golden. She dabbed the corner of her mouth with a linen napkin, then turned to the boy beside her. Her voice, though soft, carried across the candlelit table.

Across the table, Nan's eyes misted. Mossy reached for her hand and gave it a quiet squeeze.

A group of pixies flitted through the chandelier, trailing glitter behind them.

And in that hush—full of pie and satisfaction, of strangers who didn't feel so strange anymore—the house seemed to exhale. Content at last.

"You made a wish for someone you didn't know. And that wish changed everything. Thank you, Ollie."

Ollie, cheeks flaming, squirmed in his chair and stared fiercely at his plate. "It wasn't a big deal," he mumbled. "I just wanted her to wake up."

But everyone had stilled.

Nan saw it ripple through them—that tightening in the chest, that welling of tears behind the eyes. Mabel reached across and patted Ollie's hand. The Shapiro Sisters dabbed at their eyes with matching handkerchiefs, though they immediately began critiquing the sugar content in the pie.

Rufus stood with a heroic wobble, brandishing his fork like a saber. "Rematch. Tomorrow morning. No monkey paws. Just your doom."

Mildred snorted. "We'll serve your bruised backside on a silver platter—with a side of humility."

Gladys cracked her knuckles and leaned in. "Hope your donut cushion's flame-retardant, champ. 'Cause tomorrow we're roasting that rumpus."

Nan gave Mossy a wink over the rim of her wineglass. He grinned.

As the candles burned lower and plates emptied, a quietness settled. Eleanor mentioned her flight—booked for later that evening. Others echoed her plans, checking weather apps and rideshare times.

Mossy stepped behind Nan's chair and gently placed a hand on her shoulder.

"Another little bit of magic enjoyed within these walls," he murmured.

Nan's eyes stayed on the glowing pumpkins, the drowsing pixies curled like commas in their gourds, the silverware scattered like stardust.

"I wished the house would be full," she said softly. "And it was. Every room, every chair... filled with noise and stories and laughter. Now they're leaving, and still... I feel full. Isn't that strange?"

Mossy leaned down and kissed the top of her head. "Not strange at all," he said. "Even the briefest connections can change us. When you open the door to someone, even just for the shortest of times, they leave something behind. And maybe we send something with them, too."

Nan reached up and squeezed his hand. "You, Mossy dear, are my deepest wish granted."

Mossy's breath caught. "If I had a thousand wishes, in a thousand lifetimes, every wish, every breath, would be for you."

Bourbon, Bulldogs, and Goodbyes

The late afternoon light slanted through the mullioned windows of Mossy's study, gilding the dust motes. Outside, the garden glistened in the aftermath of rain, and the weeping willow waved its leafy arms as if in farewell. Inside, the fire crackled with a lazy rhythm, and the study hummed with the unspoken promise of goodbyes.

The luggage sat obediently by the front door like well-trained hunting dogs—worn handles, colorful tags, and all. The guests had eaten their fill, their plates scraped clean of cranberry chutney and bourbon-brushed Brussels sprouts, and now they moved through the house in that slow, syrupy rhythm particular to holiday afternoons.

Mossy leaned back in his leather armchair, velvet robe tied with easy flair and a tumbler of bourbon in hand. The scent of toasted pecans drifted from the dish on the table beside him, mingling with the waxy sweetness of old books and lemon furniture polish.

Around him gathered the gentlemen. Rufus slouched with theatrics on a tufted ottoman, his donut cushion discarded no longer needed. Brent examined the remains of a bourbon pour with mild surprise. Tom relaxed, freshly showered after suitcase duty, his feet propped on a nearby footstool.

Above them, chaos unfolded.

Pixies whirled through the air like uninvited cocktail garnishes.

Brash was jousting across the desk atop a cork, wielding a toothpick like a lance. Bitter had fashioned a toga from a torn cocktail napkin and was lounging in the ashtray like a fainting duchess. Neat was perched atop the bookshelf, delivering a solemn narration in a booming tone only audible to those with ears fine-tuned to fae dramatics:

"And lo! The spirits of the wild did gather for the sacred Meeting of the Padded Menfolk…"

Rufus chuckled, watching the pixies zip through the shadows. "Are they always like this after Thanksgiving?"

Mossy tilted his glass. "At our home, chaos is less of an interruption and more of a house rule."

Rufus looked toward the window with concentration.

"They're training, you know. Right now. At Pictona. Sweatbands blazing. I bet Mildred's serve hits 40 mph."

Brent raised a brow.

"They're on the court as we speak," Rufus muttered. "Hitting balls at scarecrows. Practicing voodoo."

Mossy shook his head. "Relax your glutes, Rufus. The match isn't until Tuesday."

"*You* can rest," Rufus grumbled. "They already broke *me* once. My coccyx has PTSD."

Pixie Bitter made a sympathetic wail from the ashtray and pretended to faint again.

The TV in the corner droned on with soft commentary from the dog show. A well-groomed English bulldog waddled across the screen like a duchess on parade.

Brent gestured toward it with a snort. "That one? Really? I mean, he looks like a couch pillow that learned to breathe."

"Irish Wolfhound is who I would crown king," Mossy declared, lifting his glass in solemnity. "Tall, gentle, poetic. Like a sonnet made flesh."

"Yorkie," Rufus argued. "Small. Determined. Often underestimated. Also has emotional hair."

Tom considered for a moment. "I'd pick the Labrador. Loyal, a little chaotic, and constantly hungry."

Brent grinned. "The true winner is the Chow Chow. Looks fluffy but harbors deep suspicion of strangers. Very on-brand."

Pixie Neat held up a sugar cube and declared, "The winner is the schnauzer with the side part!" before promptly falling into Mossy's glass.

Nan's voice called in musical tones, "Mossy! There is a car here. Would you be a dear and fetch our guests from the garden?"

Mossy rose with slow grace, tucking his velvet robe around him like a cloak.

"Gentlemen," he said with a nod. "It appears I am summoned to the realm of sunshine and small feet. Tom, it seems your ride is here."

Brent stretched and reached for his phone.

"Kiki wants to get to the airport early anyway. Says we might get upgraded if she works her magic. That usually means telling the check-in agent she's an influencer with an urgent skincare reveal."

"I'll pray for the airline," Mossy intoned, sweeping toward the door.

Rufus raised his bourbon. "To soft landings and no ghost stowaways."

Tom, rising as well, sighed fondly. "To strange little houses that make you believe in wishes and miracles."

Mossy turned at the door with one last glance at the pixies

tumbling over the bookshelf, the laughter curling like smoke through the firelit room.

"May your flights be smooth, your backs unbroken, and your hearts filled with wishes. Even the odd ones. Especially those."

They clinked glasses in farewell. "Funny, isn't it?" Mossy mused. "We chase wishes like they're fireflies, but gratitude stands still, quietly shining."

Rufus tilted his head. "Sounds like you swallowed a fortune cookie, buddy."

Brent laughed, "Or wrote one."

Outside, the garden echoed with the joyous laughter of children, vibrant and golden, in a world touched with enchantment and a hint of magic.

All Wishes Tucked Away

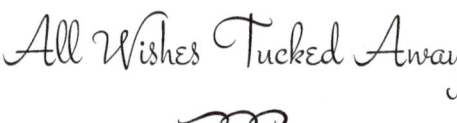

The goodbyes began with snack bags and smiles. Nan knelt in the entryway, ribbon-tied pouches in hand, her pearls catching the morning light as she offered Bea and Ollie their parting treats.

"Roasted pumpkin seeds," she said with a wink. "Half dusted with cinnamon sugar, half coated in sea salt and smoked paprika. Pick your adventure."

Bea gasped with delight and clutched hers like treasure. Ollie examined his as if weighing tactical decisions. "Can I mix them?"

"That's the bold path," Nan said.

Behind her, Mabel emerged from the parlor with a floral tin. "And something sweet to go with it. Mimosa butter cookies—dusted in orange zest and powdered sugar. They'll vanish quickly if you're not careful."

Bea squealed. Ollie solemnly nodded. "I'll guard them with my life."

Nan leaned in and kissed the top of his head. "And if I ever need anything caught again, I know just who to call."

"Deal," Ollie said, stuffing the snack bag into his backpack. "Especially if there's cookies."

Kiki and Brent's car idled just beyond the gates, their luggage already tucked in the trunk. Brent gave a final wave from the driver's side while Kiki leaned out the window, snapping a photo of the B&B's ivy-draped sign. "Tagging you now," she called. "Magical Thanksgiving at Nettles B&B. Hashtag: Miracles and Mimosa Cookies!"

Nan chuckled. "Safe travels, you two. I'll follow you online, Kiki!"

From the second waiting car, Susan was already buckling Bea in as Tom adjusted the booster seat. Ollie turned back for one last wave.

"Tell the pixies bye!"

A flicker of wings answered from the porch eaves.

Across the circular drive, a sleek black car waited for Eleanor. She stood beside it in a plum sweater set, her small leather bag in one hand and her phone glowing in the other.

Nan stepped forward, arms open. "Will you text when you get there?"

Eleanor nodded, then folded into the hug with unexpected fierceness. "She asked for something sweet," she whispered. "Said the hospital stuff tastes like glue."

Nan chuckled despite her emotions. "Then sweet she shall have," she said, placing a bag of sweets into Eleanor's hand.

They pulled apart, and Mossy kissed Eleanor's hand. "Safe roads and soft skies, dear lady."

Eleanor's eyes shimmered. She got into the car, and as it pulled down the gravel path she lowered the window and called back to Ollie:

"Thank you!"

Ollie smiled, one hand on the monkey paw in his back pocket. "You're welcome!" he replied as he waved.

The car disappeared past the double fountains, their gentle spray catching the late afternoon sun like diamonds on parade.

Just inside the door, Bithia and Cordelia stood half-shadowed near the parlor archway. Cordelia watched the road thoughtfully.

"Strange, isn't it? That an ancient curse would wait all this time for the wish of a child."

Bithia's voice was soft. "Not strange. Right. The paw needed a heart unclouded by want."

Cordelia sniffed. "Makes you wonder what else waits in that trunk."

Mabel passed by with a stack of dessert plates. "All of them, I hope, are as ready to leave as that one. I'll be in the kitchen, wrestling the gravy boat into submission."

Nan squeezed her arm as she went.

And then it was just Nan and Mossy on the front porch, the wind carrying hints of roasted rosemary and orange peel as the house settled into its late-afternoon hush.

Mossy had wrapped a soft plaid shawl around his wife's shoulders and now sat beside her on the swing, their mugs of spiced cider warm in hand.

"It was full," Nan said, gazing at the now-empty driveway.

"Bursting," Mossy agreed.

"I wished for that," she murmured. "For this house to be full. With laughter, and people, and stories."

Mossy glanced at her, smiling gently. "And it was granted, and I suspect 'twill always be the case. Every guest, even if we know them only briefly, leaves a part of themselves here, in this house."

"Like echoes," Nan added.

"Or imprints on the heart."

The porch swing creaked gently. A pixie flew past with a maple leaf for a cape.

Mossy leaned in close, brushing her temple with a kiss.

She turned to him, brows raised. "Seriously, what is your deepest wish?"

His smile turned mischievous. "Always you, Nan. From the moment I saw you in that ridiculous lavender hat, waving a garden trowel like a sabre."

Nan laughed, blinking away a sudden prickle behind her eyes. "And I, you. Even when you quoted Byron at a pancake breakfast."

"Romance comes in many forms. Syrup-drenched is one of them."

They sat in silence for a while, the late sun casting golden lacework through the porch railing. The pixies had vanished to whatever nap-time nook they fancied. The house felt still—not hollow, but hushed. Content.

Nan rose slowly, setting her empty mug down on the railing. Mossy followed, stretching his back with a groan.

And then—just as they reached the front door—Nan paused.

From upstairs, faint but unmistakable, came the low, haunted moan of a cello string.

Just one long, lonely note.

They both froze.

Nan turned, gaze lifting toward the attic stairwell.

Mossy said nothing, only laid a hand on her shoulder.

The breeze caught a curl of her hair as the final autumn leaf tumbled across the porch and came to rest at her feet.

And in a room filled with forgotten things, something old and lovely was waking up.

 A Note from Nan Nettles' Kitchen

Dear reader—may I offer you something sweet?

The story may be ending for now, but the magic of this house lingers long after the suitcases roll away and the pixies return to their naps. And here at the Nettles B&B, magic is often baked right into the crust.

If you've ever found yourself at our table during the holidays, you've likely been handed a warm plate, a second helping, and maybe a third—especially if Mabel had anything to say about it. Many of the recipes I serve to guests (and occasionally to ghosts) come straight from Teresa Sebring's cookbooks.

Teresa is a dear friend of the B&B—and a wizard with butter, spice, and joy. When the kitchen grows quiet and I find myself craving comfort—or inspiration—I often reach for her pages. Hers are the recipes I trust when planning a holiday menu, cheering up a neighbor, or simply filling the house with the scent of cinnamon and laughter.

So, I asked if she'd be willing to share some of her favorites with you here—recipes I serve at our autumn table, under flickering candlelight, on vintage china, with friends old and new gathered close.

Now it's your turn.

Tie your apron. Turn the page. Whether you're baking for guests or just for the joy of it, may these recipes bring warmth to your kitchen, kindness to your gatherings, and a little bit of Nettles magic to your day.

With mums, magic, and cinnamon skies,

Nan Nettles
Proprietress of the Nettles B&B, Daytona Beach
(*and devoted admirer of Teresa's cranberry chutney*)

A Season of Warmth

Welcome to my Autumn kitchen. Fall has always been one of my favorite seasons- it's a time to gather around the comfort of a well-loved table, creating countless fond memories of warmth, family, and food throughout the years. Even here in sunny Florida, where "fall" might mean just a slight dip in humidity and the occasional cooler breeze, I still love all those classic Autumn flavors and the feeling of the season.

These dishes are inspired by family, elevated by my time at culinary school, blended with Autumn's bounty, and infused with the sheer joy of transforming simple local ingredients into something amazing. From the earthy goodness of roasted vegetables to the sweet spices of cinnamon and pumpkin, these are dishes that I turn to when I want to gather my own family close. My hope is that these recipes will not only inspire you to cook but also help you to create your own cozy moments this fall. May your home be filled with laughter, your table with goodness, and your heart with love.

Teresa Sebring

Part One

Appetizers, Nibbles, and Welcoming Bites

There's nothing quite like the anticipation of a meal, and an appetizer is the perfect way to kick off that delicious journey. They aren't just small bites to tantalize the appetite; they're the gentle invitation to gather, to share, and to savor the moment with family and friends.

MY KITCHEN TIPS:

Before you even reach for your first pan, embrace the timeless French practice of "Miese en Place" meaning "everything in its place". Simply put, to get everything ready before you start-slicing and dicing your veggies, measuring your spices, chopping your herbs, and just having everything you need at the ready before you start cooking. It's like setting the stage for a delightful performance; making the actual cooking feel more relaxed, less rushed, and truly enjoyable. It's a little act of kindness that you can do for your future self, promising a smoother, cozier cooking experience!

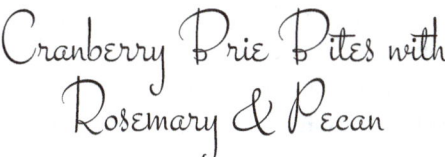

Cranberry Brie Bites with Rosemary & Pecan

These lovely little bites are a delightful explosion of festive flavors, perfect for any gathering. Warm, gooey Brie melts around tart cranberry, all nestled in a flaky pastry. Add a sprinkle of fresh rosemary and crunchy pecans and you have an aromatic, earthy finish, creating an irresistible bite.

Ingredients:

- One can crescent rolls or sheets
- One 8oz wheel of Brie
- 8oz cranberry sauce (homemade is best)
- Approx. 1/4 cup toasted pecans, chopped
- Fresh rosemary sprigs- minced 1- 2 sprigs & dividing the rest into 24 small sprigs

Directions:

1. Preheat oven to 375°, spray mini muffin tin with non-stick baking spray.
2. On a lightly floured surface roll crescent dough out slightly, making sure that any seams have been pinched closed.

3. Cut dough into 24 equal squares and Brie into 24 equal portions.
4. Place 1dough square into each muffin cup and prick several times with a fork.
5. Place a portion of Brie into each cup, top with a spoonful of cranberry sauce, and sprinkle with chopped pecans & minced rosemary.
6. Bake for 18-20 minutes, garnish with sprigs of rosemary.

Sweet Potato Crostini with Pomegranate

These Sweet little crostini offer a perfect blend of sweet and savory. It's a simple yet elegant bite, bursting with color and fresh flavor.

Ingredients:
- 2 large narrow sweet potatoes
- olive oil
- salt and pepper
- 2 tsp dried parsley
- 1 tsp dried thyme
- 2 oz cream cheese
- ¼ cup pomegranate arils
- 2 Tbsp honey, local is best

Directions:

1. Peel sweet potatoes and slice into 1/4-inch-thick slices, a mandolin works very well here.
2. Season sweet potatoes with salt and pepper and toss in olive oil to coat. On a parchment lined

baking sheet, bake at 350° for approximately 10-15 minutes until soft and golden.

3. Blend cream cheese with herbs, salt and pepper.
4. Top sweet potatoes with a dollop of cream cheese mixture, pomegranates, and drizzle with honey.

Cherry Tomato Bites

These amazing little bites are bursting with flavor- from the saltiness of the bacon to the creamy bit of goat cheese, they are like tiny little BLT's that you will come back to again and again.

Ingredients:
- 2 pints of fresh cherry tomatoes
- 8 oz mild goat cheese, softened
- 6-8 strips bacon
- ¼ cup finely sliced green onion
- ¼ cup chopped fresh parsley
- salt and black pepper to taste
- ¼ tsp Worcestershire sauce
- dash of lemon juice

Directions:

1. Cook and crumble bacon, set aside to cool.
2. With a paring knife, slice off the top of each

tomato and scoop out the seeds. Slice a small bit from the bottoms so that they sit flat.

3. Blend goat cheese, bacon, herbs, Worcestershire sauce, and lemon juice. If too thick, add a little of milk or cream.

4. Place filling into a piping bag with star tips or zip top bag with the corner snipped off, and pipe into each tomato.

Kumquat Marmalade Crostini

I love kumquats and have fond memories of eating them straight off the tree as a child, so it's no wonder that I love these sweet and salty, creamy and crunchy little bites! You'll find yourself making extra marmalade to serve over warm buttermilk biscuits with a cup of pear & ginger green tea.

Ingredients:
- 1 lb kumquats, quartered and seeded
- juice and zest of one lemon
- 1 ½ cup sugar
- 1 ½ cup water
- Ricotta cheese
- French baguette

Directions:

1. Place kumquats in a heavy saucepan with lemon juice, zest, and water. Tie seeds in a loose sachet of cheesecloth and add to pot, as they will help to thicken the marmalade.

2. Simmer for 25 to 30 minutes, stirring occasionally. Add sugar and stir to dissolve. Bring to a rolling boil and continue to cook for 15 minutes.
3. Remove seeds and allow to cool. If not using immediately seal in an airtight container.
4. Thinly sliced baguette, brush with olive oil, and toast until golden.
5. Top toasted baguette slices with ricotta cheese and marmalade.

Pumpkin & Caramelized Onion Puffs

These delectable puffs are a savory and subtly sweet treat, perfect for autumn entertaining. Flaky pastry encases the earthiness of pumpkin and meets the deep, sweet notes of caramelized onions, creating a delightful and comforting bite.

My kitchen tips: All or parts of this can very easily be made ahead!

The puff pastry can be thawed, cut, and stored in the refrigerator between sheets of parchment, and the caramelized onions can also be premade up to 2 days in advance- just bring them to room temperature before mixing with the other filling ingredients.

You can also fully assemble and store without egg wash in the refrigerator for up to 2 days, while your oven is preheating simply brush with egg wash and bake.

And finally, great caramelized onions take time and patience. If they are becoming dry during cooking, add a little water. Sprinkle with a dash of salt and sugar to bring out the natural sweetness of the onion. And try deglazing your pan with a little balsamic vinegar or red wine just before they are done to add an extra depth of flavor.

Ingredients:

- 2 cups pumpkin puree, fresh or canned (see the fresh Seminole pumpkin puree in the desert section!)
- one sheet of frozen puffed pastry
- 1 large sweet onion, thinly sliced
- ½ tsp nutmeg
- ¼ tsp sage
- one egg beaten

Directions:

1. Thaw puff pastry in the refrigerator overnight for best results. When ready to use, place on a non-stick or lightly floured surface, roll out slightly - just enough to smooth out any seams. Cut into 12 equal squares and place back into the refrigerator to keep chilled- this will promote that lovely rise and flaky texture that you want from puff pastry.
2. Cook your onions on medium to low heat in a lightly oiled sauté pan until they have developed a rich browned color. Don't rush the process - you want browned and caramelized, not burnt.
3. Assemble the filling by adding the pumpkin puree and spices to your onions and mix thoroughly. Allow to cool completely before proceeding.
4. To create your puffs, place an equal portion of filling into the center of each square. Bring opposite corners of the pastry to the center and pinch the seams to close.
5. Brush tops with egg wash and place into a

preheated 400° oven for approximately 18 to 20 minutes until pastry is golden brown.

Autumn Harvest Chicken Skewers

These skewers offer a delightful blend of savory chicken, sweet potatoes, and tart apples, all infused with a rich honey-balsamic marinade. The combination creates a perfect balance of flavors and textures, making each bite an exciting experience.

Ingredients:
- 1 lb. chicken thighs, deboned
- 2 sweet potatoes
- 2 apples
- 1 red onion
- ¼ c Olive oil
- 2 Tbsp maple syrup
- 2 Tbsp balsamic vinegar
- 1 tsp rosemary
- 1 tsp thyme
- 1 tsp nutmeg
- ½ cup apple juice

Directions:

1. In a mixing bowl prepare the marinade by combining the olive oil, maple syrup, balsamic vinegar, and herbs.
2. Cut the chicken thighs into bite-size pieces, place into a small zip top bag with approximately 1/3 of the marinade, or enough to fully coat it. Place in the refrigerator and marinade for a minimum of 1 hour, up to overnight.
3. Prepare the onion, sweet potatoes, and apples by peeling and cutting into even bite size pieces.
4. Place into a separate zip top bag with remaining marinade.
5. When ready to cook, preheat oven to 400°, prepare one or more baking sheets with cooking spray- enough to ensure that items can be spread into a single layer.
6. Place chicken and fruit/ vegetable mix onto baking sheets, keeping in mind that the different components will have different cooking times. Discard chicken marinade and reserve marinade from the fruit/ vegetable mixture.
7. Cook until each component has reached desired doneness- the sweet potato and chicken will take 20 to 30 minutes; the apple and onions will take considerably less time.
8. Meanwhile, place apple juice and reserved marinade in a small saucepan and reduce by half to create a glaze.
9. When cool enough to handle, skewer one of each apple, chicken, onion, and sweet potato and drizzle with glaze.

Cinnamon Glazed Pecans

Sweet, crunchy and aromatic with the warm spices of cinnamon and vanilla, these lovely little gems are one of those addictive snacks that you can't eat just one of- and they also top off a crisp autumn salad perfectly.

Ingredients:
- 2 cups pecan halves
- ½ cup brown sugar
- 2 tsp cinnamon
- ½ tsp salt
- ½ tsp vanilla bean extract
- 2 Tbsp orange juice

Directions:

1. Line a baking sheet with parchment paper or a silicone baking mat.
2. In a large non-stick saucepan or skillet heat all ingredients except pecans over medium heat until sugar is fully dissolved.

3. Add pecans and stir to coat.
4. Continue to stir as the sugar mixture coats the pecans and it becomes crystallized and shiny.
5. Immediately pour on prepared baking sheet to cool, taking care to spread into a single layer.
6. Once cooled, break into small pieces and store in an airtight container. Do not refrigerate.

Roasted Pumpkin Seeds

No matter the weather, we know it's Fall when the pumpkins begin to adorn the porches and the fragrance of roasting pumpkin seeds wafts through the house. There are so many ways to enjoy them, and here are two of my favorites.

Savory ingredients:
- 2 cups raw pumpkin seeds
- 1 ½ Tbsp butter, melted
- 1 ½ tsp worcestershire sauce
- 1 ¼ tsp seasoned salt

Sweet ingredients:
- 2 cups raw pumpkin seeds
- 1 ½ Tbsp butter, melted
- ½ tsp vanilla
- 2 Tbsp sugar
- 1 tsp cinnamon

Directions:

1. Rinse seeds and remove any remaining bits of pumpkin, soak in clean water overnight, up to 1 week.
2. Preheat oven to 250°
3. Drain seeds from water and pat dry, spread out on lightly greased baking sheet and bake for 20 minutes.
4. Mix butter and remaining ingredients.
5. Remove seeds from oven and toss in butter mixture, return to oven and bake until golden, approximately 30 minutes.

Cheesy Datil Brussel Sprout Dip

I love this amazing dip; it's my newest hot appetizer obsession. If you like a little spice and you're a fan of spinach artichoke dip (or any baked dip for that matter), this one needs to be on your menu this year! Datil peppers are a local flavor of the St. Augustine area, with a sweet flavor but heat level around the habanero. Adjust the amount you use to your taste preferences.

Ingredients:
- 1 lb brussels sprouts
- 3 cloves garlic, minced
- 1 shallot, minced
- ¾ cup mayonnaise
- ¾ cup sour cream
- ½ datil pepper, ribs and seeds removed, minced
- 2 Tbsp lemon juice
- salt & pepper
- 2 cups total of a combination of any of the following-shredded mozzarella, Monterey Jack, sharp cheddar, or an Italian blend

Direction:

1. Preheat oven to 350°
2. Slice the Brussels sprouts thinly, discarding the stems. Set aside.
3. Put the garlic, shallot, mayo, sour cream, pepper, lemon juice, salt, and pepper into the bowl of a food processor. Pulse a few times, then process briefly until smooth. It will still have some texture.
4. Add the cheeses and pulse to combine. The longer you process the smoother the texture will be.
5. Fold the Brussel sprouts into the cheese mixture and spread into a shallow baking dish. Bake for 40-45 minutes, until bubbling and just beginning to brown on top- make sure that the center is good and hot.
6. Serve immediately with crusty bread, pita or tortilla chips, veggies, the possibilities are endless!

Sun Dried Tomato and Pumpkin Seed Pesto Dip

It's fall and all the fresh tomatoes of summer are gone, but that's not going to stop us from making an amazing dip bursting with sweet tomato flavor. Instead, we are going to pair it up with a bright pesto made from earthy pumpkin seeds and ooey- gooey cheesy goodness. Grab your baguette because once you dig in you won't want to stop.

Ingredients:
- ¾ cups fresh pumpkin seed pesto, recipe to follow
- 2 8 oz packages cream cheese, softened
- 2 cups sun dried tomatoes, julienned
- 2 cups parmesan cheese, freshly grated
- 16 oz sour cream
- 4 roasted garlic cloves, mashed
- ½ tsp each dried basil, oregano, and thyme
- fresh baguette, torn into small chunks for serving

Directions:

1. Preheat oven to 350°

2. Mix the pesto and 1 block of the cream cheese. Spread onto the bottom of an 8x8 baking dish.
3. In a separate bowl, blend together the remaining block of cream cheese and the rest of the ingredients, and spread evenly over the pesto mixture.
4. Bake for 25-30 minutes, or until bubbly and beginning to brown on top. Garnish with additional sun-dried tomatoes, fresh basil, and toasted pumpkin seeds. Allow to cool slightly before serving warm with fresh bread.

Pumpkin Seed Pesto

Ingredients:
- ½ cup shelled pumpkin seeds, roasted
- 3 Tbsp freshly grated parmesan cheese
- 2 cloves garlic (for a more rustic flavor use roasted garlic)
- ¾ cups basil leaves
- ¾ cups spinach leaves
- 2 Tbsp lemon juice
- ½-¾ cup olive oil
- Salt to taste

Directions:

1. Combine pumpkin seeds, parmesan, and garlic in the bowl of a food processor. Pulse on and off until it begins to form a paste and seeds are ground.
2. Add basil, spinach and lemon juice and begin to pulse. Slowly drizzle in the olive oil until all

ingredients are combined. Be careful to not over-process, you want your basil and spinach to remain bright, and you do not want it to be too thin- it should resemble more of a loose paste than a sauce.

Datil Shrimp Dip

If you are looking for something a little different, look no more. This creamy dip is spicy and flavorful, featuring succulent shrimp and the unique, fruity heat of St. Augustine's Datil peppers. This distinctive dip offers a balance of sweet and hot, making it a zesty choice for seafood enthusiasts who enjoy a kick.

Ingredients:
- ½ lb. shrimp
- ¼ cup mayonnaise
- ¼ cup sour cream
- ½ cup cream cheese
- ¼ cup thinly sliced green onion
- juice of one lemon
- 1 Tbsp seafood seasoning
- 2 tsp minced fresh parsley
- 1 tsp minced fresh thyme
- datil pepper hot sauce, to taste
- salt and pepper

Directions:

1. Peel, devein, and cook shrimp. Once cool, dice into small pieces.
2. In a large bowl mix all other ingredients well, carefully fold in diced shrimp. Adjust seasoning to taste with hot sauce, salt, and pepper. Chill for at least 1 hour before serving.
3. Serve with an assortment of fresh vegetables and crackers.

Part Two

Bread and Biscuits, Warm from the Oven

There's something amazing about the aroma of freshly baked bread filling the kitchen. Breads are about warmth, home, and the simple magic of flour transforming into something utterly delicious. From a fluffy biscuit soaking up the last bit of hearty stew, to a rustic loaf slathered with butter, they truly anchor a cozy fall meal and turn it into a moment to remember.

MY KITCHEN TIPS:

For truly tender biscuits and moist quick breads, remember that a light hand is your friend. Once you have combined your wet and dry ingredients, mix just until it starts to come together- in fact a few lumps in your batter is desirable. While over mixing will lead to tough, dry, and dense results, your gentle touch will reward you with a soft and tender crumb that melts in your mouth.

Orange Cranberry Pecan Bread

Get ready to slice into a taste of sunshine! This sweet, fragrant quick bread is bursting with the zing of Florida's favorite citrus balanced with tart fall cranberries & crunchy pecans for a wonderfully moist and undeniably delicious treat. It's so easy you'll be making it all the time, no matter the weather or time of year.

Ingredients:
- 2 cups all-purpose flour
- 1 cup sugar
- 1 ½ tsp baking soda
- ½ tsp salt
- 1 egg
- ½ cup orange juice
- zest of 1 orange
- ½ cup plain yogurt
- 2 Tbsp vegetable oil
- 2 Tbsp hot water
- 1 cup fresh or frozen cranberries- thaw and drain if using frozen

- 1 cup pecans, roughly chopped

Directions:

1. Preheat oven to 350° and use pan spray to grease a standard loaf pan.
2. In a large bowl, mix all ingredients and pour into loaf pan.
3. Bake for 70 minutes until golden brown on top. Cool in the pan on a wire rack for about an hour before removing and slicing.

Classic Sweet Cornbread with Maple & Datil Pepper Variations

There's nothing quite like the comforting aroma of a classic cornbread, a true staple on many tables. This cornbread has the perfect balance of sweetness, creating a bread that is moist, never dry, and ideal for everything from cozy dinners to weekend brunches. While delicious on its own, this versatile recipe also welcomes a few simple additions. While there are endless possibilities, here I've outlined a decadent maple variation and a spicy local Datil pepper option.

Ingredients:
- 1 cup all-purpose flour
- 1 cup yellow cornmeal
- ⅔ cup sugar
- 3 ½ tsp baking powder
- 1 tsp salt
- 1 cup milk
- ⅓ cup vegetable oil
- 1 large egg

To go Maple:
- Sub ¼ cup maple syrup for sugar

- Sub 4 Tbsp melted butter for oil
- 2 eggs instead of 1

To go Spicy:

- 1 datil pepper, roasted and finely diced
- 1 cup cheddar cheese, shredded

Directions:

1. Preheat oven to 400°. Lightly grease a 9-inch round cake pan or equivalent baking dish.
2. In a large bowl whisk together dry ingredients-flour, cornmeal, sugar, baking powder & salt.
3. Add milk, oil or butter, and egg, and whisk until well combined.
4. Stir in any additional ingredients.
5. Pour into prepared pan and bake 20-25 minutes, until a toothpick inserted into the center comes out clean.

Pumpkin Scones with Cinnamon Spice Whipped Cream

These scones are the sophisticated, slightly sweet cousin to your favorite fluffy biscuit. This is a fall- flavored twist on a classic soft & flaky scone with crumbly edges and a crunchy sugar crust. Serve with a creamy, dreamy cinnamon spiced whipped cream and teatime will never be the same.

My kitchen tip: Blotting the excess moisture from the pumpkin puree is important here. Pumpkin has a lot of moisture- fresh even more than canned. The moister the dough, the more muffin like the texture will be. And, as delightful as muffins are- that's not what we are going for here! We want our scones to be flaky and crumbly, not super moist and muffin like.

Ingredients:
- 2 cup all-purpose flour
- 2 1/2 tsp baking powder
- 1 tsp ground cinnamon
- 1 ½ tsp pumpkin pie spice
- ½ tsp salt

- ½ cup unsalted butter, frozen
- ⅓ cup 2 Tbsp heavy cream, divided
- 1 large egg
- ½ cup fresh or canned pumpkin puree, blotted*
- ½ cup dark brown sugar, packed
- 1 tsp vanilla extract
- Coarse sugar for sprinkling on top before baking

Directions:

1. Preheat the oven to 400°. Line two baking sheets with parchment paper.
2. In a large bowl whisk together all the dry ingredients- flour, baking powder, cinnamon, pumpkin pie spice, and salt.
3. Cut the frozen butter into small pieces. Add to the flour mixture and combine with a pastry cutter or 2 forks to evenly cut the butter into the dry ingredients, you want it to be crumbly and have no larger than pea sized bits of butter.
4. In a separate bowl, whisk together heavy cream, egg, pumpkin, brown sugar, and vanilla. Pour over the flour mixture and quickly and gently mix all together, until no dry streaks remain. Take care to avoid over- mixing here.
5. Turn the mixture out onto a flour-dusted surface and gently knead a few times until it holds together and can form a ball (it is good to dust your hands with flour before kneading as the dough will be sticky). Press the dough flat into an 8-in disc and with a sharp knife cut into eight equal pie wedges.
6. Place wedges at least 2 inches apart on the prepared baking sheet(s). At this point you may

want to place them in the refrigerator/ freezer for up to 15 minutes, depending on how warm your kitchen is. Before baking, use a pastry brush to brush the dough with the remaining heavy cream and sprinkle with coarse sugar.

7. Bake for 20 minutes until lightly browned.

Cinnamon Spiced Whipped Cream

Ingredients:
- 1 cup heavy cream
- 3 Tbsp powdered (confectioners) sugar
- ½ tsp cinnamon or pumpkin pie spice
- 1 tsp vanilla

Directions:

1. In the bowl of a stand mixer with a whisk attachment (or hand mixer) beat the heavy whipping cream until you have soft peaks. Add sugar, cinnamon or pie spice, and vanilla, and continue to beat until everything is fully incorporated and you have stiff peaks. Taste and adjust seasoning as needed.

Rosemary Honey Rolls

Dinner rolls, that little piece of bread at so many meals that is often an afterthought. But what if it was a soft, pillowy cloud of goodness instead? Perfumed with the earthy scent of rosemary and touched with a sweet kiss of honey, these rolls may take more time than a store-bought pack of generic dinner rolls, but they are well worth the effort, transforming a simple side into a memorable highlight.

Ingredients:
- 1 cup water
- ½ cup milk
- 2 Tbsp unsalted butter
- 2 Tbsp honey
- 1 Tbsp active dry yeast (this is a little more than 1 package)
- 3 ½ -4 cups all-purpose flour
- 1 tsp salt
- 1 Tbsp fresh rosemary, finely chopped
- 1 tsp garlic powder
- 1 egg + 1 tsp milk, beaten together for egg wash

- coarse sea salt to top

Directions:

1. In a heavy saucepan stir together the water, milk, butter, and honey. Heat the mixture over medium low heat, stirring occasionally, until butter is melted and it reaches 110°.
2. Pour the mixture into the bowl of a stand mixer. Sprinkle the yeast on top and set aside to allow yeast to activate until it forms a creamy foam, anywhere from 5- 15 minutes.
3. Fit mixer with a dough hook attachment. To the yeast mixture add in 3 cups of the flour, salt, rosemary and garlic powder. Mix on low speed until no dry spots remain. Continue to add remaining flour a few tablespoons at a time (no more than 4 cups total, you may not need all the flour), until a firm dough forms that pulls away from the sides of the bowl and is only slightly sticky to the touch. Increase speed to medium low and knead until elastic and smooth, about 4-6 minutes.
4. Transfer dough to a bowl that has been greased with olive oil, turning it to coat. Cover loosely with plastic wrap or a damp towel and let rise in a warm spot until it has doubled in size, about an hour.
5. Preheat oven to 375°and line a baking sheet with parchment paper.
6. Gently punch the dough down and transfer to a work surface. Divide into between 15 & 30 equal sized pieces, depending on the size roll that you prefer. Form each piece into a ball, pinching the

seams on the underside to create a smooth round top.

7. Transfer dough balls to prepared baking sheet, placing them close together but not touching. Brush tops lightly with egg wash and sprinkle with sea salt. Cover and let rise in a warm place until nearly doubled, about 20 minutes

8. Uncover and bake for 15- 20 minutes until golden brown. Serve with compound honey butter.

HOMEMADE HONEY BUTTER

Ingredients:
- 1 cup (2 sticks) unsalted butter, softened to room temperature
- 6 Tbsp local honey
- 1 ½ tsp salt

Directions:

1. Put butter, honey and salt in the bowl of a stand mixer fitted with a whisk attachment. Mix on medium speed until fully combined, smooth, and creamy. Taste for seasoning and adjust to taste. Alternatively, this can easily be done in a small bowl with a hand mixer.

Cranberry Sauce Muffins

Much like the Cranberry Bars in the desert section, I originally came up with these quick and easy muffins to use up leftover cranberry sauce after thanksgiving. Then they became part of the thanksgiving meal. Then I found myself making extra cranberry sauce and freezing it just so I could make these any time! Yeah, they're just that good.

Ingredients:
- 2 cups all-purpose flour
- ½ cups dark brown sugar, packed
- ¼ cups sugar
- 1 Tbsp baking powder
- ½ tsp salt
- ½ tsp cinnamon
- ¼ tsp nutmeg
- ¼ tsp clove
- 1 cup cranberry sauce
- ¾ cup milk
- ¼ cup vegetable oil
- 1 egg

- 1 tsp vanilla extract

Directions:

1. Preheat oven to 400°and prepare muffin tin with liners (batter should make around 18 muffins).
2. In a large bowl whisk together the flour, sugars, baking powder, and spices.
3. In a separate bowl blend the rest of the ingredients together. Gently stir dry ingredients into the wet and mix just until moistened.
4. Scoop into prepared muffin cups and bake 20 minutes, until golden on top.

Chocolate Chip Pumpkin Bread

Singing with the warm spices of autumn and studded with the irresistible allure of warm melty chocolate, you will adore this classic quick bread. It's a truly cozy treat- ideal for breakfast or just curling up with a good book and a warm cup of tea.

Ingredients:
- 2 cups fresh pumpkin puree (or 1 15oz. can)
- 1 cup vegetable or olive oil
- 1 cup sugar
- 1 cup dark brown sugar, packed
- 4 eggs
- ½ tsp cinnamon
- ½ tsp grated nutmeg
- ½ tsp allspice
- ½ tsp ground ginger
- 2 ¾ cups all-purpose flour
- 1 tsp salt
- 2 tsp baking soda
- 1 cup pecans or walnuts, roughly chopped- optional
- 10 oz good quality dark chocolate chips

Directions:

1. Preheat oven to 350° Use pan spray to grease a standard loaf pan.
2. Whisk together the pumpkin, oil sugars, eggs and spices.
3. In a separate bowl whisk together the flour, salt, & baking soda.
4. Gently stir dry ingredients into the wet and mix until just combined. Fold in the nuts and chocolate chips.
5. Pour into the loaf pan and bake for about minutes until the loaf is fully risen and starting to crack on top, or until a toothpick inserted near the center comes out clean.
6. Cool on a wire rack about an hour.

Cinnamon Swirl Bread

Time and patience are the keys here. The reward is the most amazingly tender, mouthwatering, cinnamony sweet loaf that you have ever had the pleasure to make. Try slicing it thick and making French toast with it for breakfast, or just do what I prefer and have it warm with just a little slathering of butter. Either way the most challenging part will be waiting for it to cool enough to slice!

Ingredients:
- 1 cup warm whole milk, warmed (about 110°)
- 4 Tbsp unsalted butter, softened to room temperature
- 2 Tbsp sugar
- 1 egg + 2 egg yolks, lightly beaten
- 1 envelope instant dry yeast
- 3 cups bread flour, plus more as needed
- 1 ¼ tsp salt

For the cinnamon swirl:
- 2 Tbsp unsalted butter, melted
- ¼ cup sugar
- ¼ cup brown sugar

- 2 Tbsp cinnamon

For the egg wash:

- 1 egg
- 1 Tbsp milk

Directions:

1. Fit a stand mixer with a dough hook attachment.
2. In the bowl of the stand mixer whisk together the milk, butter, sugar, eggs, and yeast.
3. Add ½ the flour and salt, and beat on low speed for about 30 seconds, scrape down the sides of the bowl with a silicone spatula and add the remaining flour. Continue to beat until a rough dough comes together and it is pulling away from the sides of the bowl. If it is still too wet to a point where kneading would be impossible, beat in more flour 1 Tbsp. at a time until you have a workable dough. Increase to medium speed for 5-10 minutes until it becomes smooth and supple. If the dough slowly bounces back when poked it is ready to rise.
4. Transfer the dough to a lightly greased large bowl, turning to coat it on all sides. Cover the bowl with plastic wrap and allow to rise in a warm environment for 1 ½- 2 hours, until puffy and almost doubled in size.
5. Grease a 9x5 inch loaf pan and whisk together the sugars and cinnamon for the swirl.
6. When the dough is ready, punch it down. Lightly flour a work surface, your hands, and rolling pin. Roll into an 8 x 20-inch rectangle- It doesn't have to be perfect, rounded edges are fine! Using a pastry brush, brush the surface with melted

butter, then sprinkle with cinnamon-sugar, leaving a 1 inch border uncovered.

7. Roll into a tight log, pinching the ends to seal and prevent filling from leaking out. Place the loaf, seam side down, into the prepared pan. Any filling that spills out can be sprinkled on top of the bread in the pan.

8. Cover the pan loosely with lightly grease plastic wrap and allow to rise for 1 hour, or until it's domed about 1 inch above the top of the pan.

9. Preheat the oven to 350° If using a glass or ceramic baking dish, drop the temperature to 325°.

10. In a small bowl beat the egg and milk, brush gently all over the top of the dough.

11. Bake on a lower position in the oven for about 45 minutes, or until golden brown. (If using a glass or ceramic dish, bake for closer to 1 hour). Check on the bread about halfway through baking- if the top is browning too quickly, tent with aluminum foil.

12. The bread is done when an instant read thermometer inserted into the center of the loaf registers at least 185°. If you gently tap on the loaf, it should sound hollow.

13. Remove from the oven and allow bread to cool completely in the pan on a wire rack before removing to slice.

14. Cover leftover bread tightly and store at room temp for up to 6 days. It can also be sliced and frozen.

Apple Pull Apart Bread

Ooey Gooey, apple cinnamony goodness is the bottom line here. This is so fun to make, and there are a lot of different ways to do it- you can go quick and easy with store bought biscuit dough or fully homemade with your own dough. Both ways work great and will give you very similar results, so I've given the variations here for you to play with.

And don't forget to play with your ingredients, too. Add nuts, change up your spices, even switch out the apples for something else (cranberries, anyone??) and most of all, just have fun with it!!

Ingredients:
For the filling:
- 2 Tbsp unsalted butter
- 3 Granny Smith apples, peeled, cored, and diced
- ½ cup dark brown sugar, packed
- 1 Tbsp ground cinnamon

For the dough:
- *1 can refrigerated biscuits*

-OR-

- *1 package frozen dinner rolls, thawed*
-OR-
- 3 cups all-purpose flour
- ¼ cups sugar
- ½ tsp salt
- 2 ¼ tsp instant dry yeast
- 4 Tbsp unsalted butter, melted
- ⅓ cup milk, warmed (about 110°F)
- ¼ cups water, warmed (about 110°F)
- 1 tsp. vanilla extract
- 2 large eggs, room temperature

For the glaze:
- 1 cup confectioner' sugar
- 1 tsp vanilla
- 3-5 tsp water

Directions:
For the filling:

1. Melt butter in a saucepan over medium heat. Add apples, brown sugar, and cinnamon and cook for about 5 minutes. Set aside.

For the dough how you proceed will depend on your preference:

1. If using frozen thawed dinner rolls, cut each roll in half. (Personally, this is my least favorite method, simply because I prefer the stacked look of the other 2 options.) Skip to step 9.
2. If using refrigerated biscuit dough, lay each biscuit out on a work surface and lightly roll out a little. Skip to step 9.
3. If making homemade dough (preferred)-

4. Whisk together the warm milk & water, melted butter, eggs and vanilla.

5. In the bowl of a stand mixer with the hook attachment whisk together flour, sugar, salt and yeast. With the mixer on low, add wet ingredients. Increase speed to medium low and knead about 2 minutes, adding more flour or water as necessary to make a smooth, soft dough.

6. Place the dough in a lightly greased bowl and cover. Allow to rest until it doubles in size, about an hour.

7. Gently punch down the dough and turn it out onto a lightly floured work surface. Roll the dough into a 12x 20-inch rectangle. (not looking for perfection here, don't forget that you're having fun)

8. Grease a 9 x5 loaf pan or 9-inch cake pan.

Assembly:

1. If using the cut dinner rolls, create an indention in each piece and place a dollop of the apple mixture in the center. Pinch the edges together and seal, forming a ball. Place ½ the balls into the prepared pan. Sprinkle in any remaining filling, and add the rest of the balls, squeezing them in tightly. Skip to step 16 to bake.

2. If using the rolled out biscuits, place an even amount of filling on top of each biscuit and stack them, a few at a time. Turn the stacks on edge and place them in the pan one in front of the other from one end of the pan to the other, squeezing them in tightly. Skip to step 16 to bake.

3. If using the homemade dough, spread the filling mixture over the surface of rolled out dough.
4. Cut the dough crosswise into six even long strips, stack the strips one on top of another, then cut the stack into six pieces.
5. Turn the pieces on edge and place them in the loaf pan one in front of the other from one end of the pan to the other, squeezing them in tightly.
6. Cover the pan and allow the loaf to rise for 30- 60 minutes, until it's almost doubled in size.
7. Preheat the oven to 350°. Bake for 45-55 minutes, tenting with foil midway if getting to dark. Cool on a wire rack for about 20 minutes to allow sugars to set before turning out onto a serving plate to cool completely.

For the glaze:

1. Whisk together the confectioners sugar, vanilla, and 3 tsp. of water. Add more water, 1 tsp. at a time until a pourable consistency. Drizzle the glaze of the cooled bread.

Savory Herbed Sausage Bread

It's hard not to go wrong when it comes to filling freshly baked bread with savory meat and melty cheese. Make your own dough or use store bought- our local grocery store stocks freshly prepared ready to use dough in the bakery, how easy is that! Try serving with marinara on the side - This would be great for a gathering, but I could totally keep it to myself and call it a meal. As with many of my recipes it's so versatile, try using different filling ingredients and herbs to make it your own.

Ingredients:
- 1 lb store bought or freshly prepared pizza dough (recipe follows)
- 1 small shallot, minced
- 2 cloves garlic, minced
- 4 oz mushrooms (cremini work well here)
- olive oil as needed
- ½ tsp each rosemary & thyme, finely chopped
- 1 tsp. flat leaf parsley, finely chopped
- 1 tsp red pepper flake, to taste

- salt & pepper
- 1 lb. Sweet or spicy Italian sausage, casings removed if needed
  - 2 cups shredded Italian blend cheese
  - 2 Tbsp unsalted butter, melted OR 1 egg, whisked
  - 1 Tbsp grated Parmesan cheese (optional)
  - 1 tsp dried Italian seasoning

Directions:

1. Preheat oven to 425°
2. In a large sauté pan over medium-high heat, heat 2 Tbsp of olive oil and cook shallots, garlic, and mushrooms until the shallots are translucent and mushrooms are lightly browned. Add herbs and spices and continue to cook for about 2 more minutes. Transfer to a bowl.
3. Add more olive oil if needed and cook sausage until browned and thoroughly cooked, stirring often and breaking it into small pieces as you go. Remove to a paper towel lined plate to drain.
4. Roll or stretch pizza dough into a roughly 13x 9 inch rectangle about ¼ inch thick. Perfection is not necessary, it's more important to have an even thickness. Don't roll it out too thin or the filling will spill out once it's rolled. If your dough is too elastic, allow to stand at room temperature for about 10 minutes to let it relax.
5. Combine mushroom mixture and sausage, and spread on top of your dough, leaving a ½ inch border around the edges. Top with shredded cheese.
6. Starting from a long side, roll the dough up tightly. Pinch to seal and tuck the ends

underneath, and position seam side down on a parchment lined baking sheet.

7. Brush with melted butter or egg, and sprinkle with parmesan cheese and Italian seasoning. Cut a few slits in the top of the dough for steam to escape.

8. Bake until golden brown and cooked through, about 30- 35 minutes. Check after 20 minutes, you may need to cover with aluminum foil to prevent over browning. Allow to cool before slicing.

Homemade Pizza Dough

Ingredients:
- ¾ cup warm water
- 1½ tsp sugar
- 1 package active dry yeast
- 2 cups all-purpose flour, plus more a needed
- 1 tsp salt
- 1 Tbsp plus 1 teaspoon extra-virgin olive oil

Directions:

1. In a small bowl, stir together the water, sugar, and the yeast. Set aside for 5 minutes, until the yeast is foamy.
2. In the bowl of a stand mixer fitted with a dough hook, place the flour and salt, and whisk to combine. Add the yeast mixture and 1 tablespoon of the olive oil. Mix on medium speed until the dough forms into a ball around the hook, 5 to 6 minutes. If the dough is too dry to form a ball, add water ½ tablespoon at a time until the mixture

comes together. If the dough is too sticky, add a little more flour.

3. Turn the dough out onto a lightly floured surface and gently knead into a smooth ball.

4. With a pastry brush, generously brush the sides of a large bowl with olive oil and place the dough inside. Use your hands to roll the dough along the inside of the bowl to coat it in olive oil. Cover the bowl tightly with plastic wrap and set aside in a warm place to rise until the dough has doubled in size, anywhere from 30 minutes to 1 hour.

5. At this point it is ready to use, either for sausage bread above or to simply make pizza.

6. Turn the dough out onto a floured surface. Stretch to fit a 14-inch pizza pan or similar.

7. Brush with olive oil and prick with a fork all over the center of the pizza to keep the dough from bubbling up in the oven. Top and bake as desired, typically 10 to 13 minutes in a 500°F oven, or until the crust is browned.

Autumn Rosemary and Herb Focaccia Bread

This beautiful bread is a fragrant, airy Italian flatbread that captures the essence of the fall season. It boasts a beautifully dimpled, olive oil-rich crust and a tender interior. Beyond the classic earthy rosemary, this autumn variation incorporates other seasonal herbs like thyme & sage, as well as caramelized onions & roasted garlic, and accented with flaky sea salt. Roasted pumpkin or other hard squash would top it nicely for an added fall boost. You'll notice that unlike most of my other breads I'm not using the stand mixer here. It's simply because this dough comes together so easily, but you can absolutely use the mixer if desired.

Ingredients:
- 2 cups lukewarm water (85° to 95°)
- 2 tsp active dry yeast
- 4 cups bread flour
- 2 to 3 tsp salt
- 2 to 3 tsp olive oil
- 2 Tbsp each chopped fresh rosemary, oregano, thyme, sage as desired

- caramelized onions and/ or roasted garlic
- 1 tsp flaky sea salt

Directions:

1. Measure the water into a large bowl. Sprinkle the yeast over the water and stir until dissolved. Stir in two cups of the flour and the salt and stir briskly until smooth, about 2 minutes. With a strong wooden or silicone spoon stir in the remaining two cups of flour for about 2 minutes longer, just until the dough pulls away from the sides of the bowl and the flour is incorporated. The dough will be fairly wet and tacky, but when it pulls away from the sides of the bowl and forms a loose ball, you'll know the dough has been stirred sufficiently. If it seems too sticky stir in an additional 1/4 to 1/2 cup of flour.

2. Cover the bowl with plastic wrap and let the dough rise in a warm place until doubled in volume, 30 to 40 minutes.

3. Grease a 9x 13-inch baking dish with olive oil and preheat the oven to 400° (if not using overnight method). Pour the dough into the dish by loosening it with a spatula and then carefully scraping it from the sides of the bowl, keeping the dough as inflated as possible. The shape that the dough takes on as it falls into the pan is fine. Set aside to rise one more time until doubled, about 15 to 20 minutes. -OR-

4. If you prefer an overnight method, cover the dish and refrigerate overnight. The dough will rise in the refrigerator and acquire flavor from the slower yeast action. Remove the dough 2 hours before

baking and let it stand, covered, in a warm place. The dough will rise a second time.

5. Once done rising, using your fingers, dimple the surface of the dough deeply and evenly (all the way to the surface of the baking pan!). Brush with olive oil and sprinkle with herbs, caramelized onion and/ or garlic.

6. Place the bread in the preheated oven and bake for approx. 25 minutes or until nicely browned and cooked through. Remove and allow to cool on a wire rack for at least 5 minutes. Garnish with any remaining herbs, flaky sea salt and a drizzle of olive oil as desired.

Classic Buttermilk Biscuits

There is just nothing like a tender, buttery biscuit; and you'll be surprised just how easy they are to whip up. As perfect alongside bacon, eggs and a cup of coffee as they are slathered with sweet homemade preserves alongside a cup of tea, each flaky bite is a taste of pure homemade comfort.

Ingredients:
- 8 oz cake flour
- 8 oz all-purpose flour
- 1 Tbsp baking powder
- ⅛ tsp baking soda
- 2 Tbsp sugar
- 1 ½ tsp salt
- 6 Tbsp (3 oz.) cold butter
- 1 cup buttermilk
- 1 cup heavy cream

Directions:

1. In a large mixing bowl whisk together flours, baking powder and soda, sugar, and salt
2. Cut the cold butter into small pieces. add to the flour mixture and combine with a pastry cutter or 2 forks to evenly cut the butter into the dry ingredients, you want it to be crumbly and have no larger than pea sized bits of butter.
3. Mix buttermilk and heavy cream together, slowly drizzle over the butter/ flour mixture and whisk together until it is all combined.
4. Transfer to a floured work surface and fold/ knead a few times, do not overwork or your biscuits will be tough instead of flaky. Pat out to a ½ inch thickness.
5. Cut out biscuits and lay on sheet pan about 2 inches apart. Bring scraps together and cut out remaining biscuits, do not repeat more than once.
6. Bake at 325° for about 10 minutes, until golden brown.

Part Three

Soups & Salads, Bowls of Warmth and Freshness

As the days begin to shorten and the Autumn light begins to glow warm and soft, there's a particular comfort found in a steaming bowl of soup or a crisp salad. Soups are a testament to how simple wholesome ingredients can, with a little love and time, create something so deeply satisfying. And an Autumn salad? Not just a side dish, but a celebration of the season's bounty- crunchy leaves, warm roasted vegetables, and tangy dressings that add a burst of life to your meal. These are the culinary version of a warm hug to give to those you care most about.

MY KITCHEN TIPS:

When you're busy prepping your "Mise en Place", especially fresh herbs and veggies, keep a bowl next to your cutting board for all your scraps and trimmings. It makes cleaning up so much quicker and your workspace tidy, leaving you more time to enjoy the delightful aromas filling your home.

Grant-Perkins Cheese Soup

A family favorite passed down from generation to generation, this comforting soup is perfect for blustery cold and busy weeknights. It is easily modified with whatever vegetables your family prefers and comes together quickly- try serving with hunks of warm crusty bread.

Ingredients:
- 2 tsp olive oil or unsalted butter
- 1 quart water
- 4 tsp roasted chicken bouillon paste
- 1 onion, diced
- 1 cup celery, diced
- 2 ½ cups potatoes, cubed
- 1 cup carrots, diced
- 1 cup small broccoli florets
- 1 cup small cauliflower florets
- 1 lb. Velveeta Cheese, cubed
- 2 cans Cream of Chicken Soup
- 1 can Cheddar Cheese Soup

Instructions:

1. In the bottom of a heavy stockpot, sauté the onion & celery until soft and lightly browned.
2. Add water and bouillon, stirring to blend completely. Add potatoes.
3. Bring to a boil and add all other vegetables, reduce heat to medium and simmer until the vegetables are just beginning to become tender.
4. Add cheese and soups and return to a simmer (do not boil). Gently simmer approx. 10 minutes, until fully blended and heated throughout.

Roasted Pumpkin Soup

A rich and hearty autumn soup that is as satisfying as it is filling. The warm spices and creamy broth will instantly transport you to a place where the leaves are ablaze with color and a crisp breeze rustles through the trees. Try making it with butternut squash or a mix, the possibilities are as tasty as they are endless.

Ingredients:
- 2 Tbsp unsalted butter
- 2 cups raw pumpkin or other winter squash diced
- salt & pepper
- 2 Tbsp olive oil
- ½ cup onion, diced
- ½ cup celery, diced
- ½ cup carrot, diced
- 1 cinnamon stick or 1 tsp ground cinnamon, toasted
- salt & pepper
- ½ tsp ground coriander, toasted
- 32 oz chicken or vegetable broth
- ½ cup heavy cream

- 2 Tbsp pumpkin seeds, toasted
- croutons, if desired

Directions:

1. Preheat oven to 375° Season squash with salt and pepper. In an oven safe sauté pan, melt butter over medium heat; add squash and sauté just until it begins to brown. Place pan in the oven and roast for approx. 15 minutes, or until browned and cooked through. Allow to cool slightly and lightly mash, you should have about 1 ½ cups.
2. In a heavy stockpot over medium heat, lightly toast the cinnamon and coriander. Add the oil and sauté onion, carrot, and celery until soft and translucent, do not brown.
3. Add the broth and bring to a gentle boil, simmering for several minutes. Stir in the squash and continue to simmer for an additional 10-15 minutes. Discard the cinnamon stick if using.
4. Remove from heat. Use an immersion blender to puree until smooth.
5. Swirl in heavy cream just before serving and top with toasted pumpkin seeds and crouton.

Turkey & Wild Rice Soup

Brothy, creamy, and easy, what could be better? This craveable twist on the classic chicken noodle soup feeds the soul and nourishes the body quickly and easily, using leftover turkey or roast chicken. Your family will think that you've been simmering all day- I won't tell if you don't!

Ingredients:
- 4 Tbsp unsalted butter
- 1 ½ cups celery, diced
- 1 ½ cups carrot, diced
- 1 onion, diced
- 3 cloves garlic, minced
- 1 ½ tsp fresh thyme, finely chopped
- 1 tsp fresh rosemary, finely chopped
- salt & pepper
- 1 bay leaf
- ¼ cup all- purpose flour
- 1 cup wild rice blend
- 4 qt chicken broth

- 4 cups leftover roasted turkey or chicken, cut into bite size pieces
- 1 cup heavy cream

Directions:

1. In a large heavy stockpot, melt butter over medium heat. Add vegetables and sauté until beginning to soften, about 5 minutes.
2. Add herbs and sprinkle with flour; stir to coat and cook 3 more minutes or until vegetables begin to brown.
3. Stirring vigorously, slowly pour in stock. Add wild rice and bring to a boil.
4. Reduce heat and simmer over medium heat for 30 minutes.
5. Add the turkey or chicken and continue to simmer for an additional 10- 15 minutes until rice and vegetables are tender.
6. Remove bay leaf, stir in cream, and season with salt and pepper to taste.

Minorcan Clam Chowder

A regional dish unique to the St. Augustine area, Minorcan Clam Chowder is a take on a classic tomato-based chowder that includes Datil peppers. Sweet & fruity but with a heat similar to the habanero, these peppers are indigenous to St. Augustine and add a distinctive kick, making Minorcan Clam Chowder truly special.

Ingredients:
- 2 lbs. clams, cooked and minced or 2 6.5oz. cans of minced clams, drained (reserve juice)
- 4 oz bacon
- 1 datil pepper, minced *
- 1 medium onion, diced
- 1 green bell pepper, diced
- 2 carrots, diced
- 3 small red potatoes, diced
- 1 15 oz can diced tomatoes
- 3 Tbsp tomato paste
- 2 cloves garlic, minced
- 1 tsp each oregano, rosemary, & thyme

- salt & pepper to taste
- 3 bay leaves
- 8 oz clam juice or reserved juice from canned clams
- 2 cups fish stock

If concerned about heat level, use ½ of a Datil pepper with seeds removed. Alternatives to fresh pepper are Datil hot sauce or dust, which can easily be ordered online.

Directions:

1. Dice bacon into small pieces and brown in a heavy stockpot. Remove bacon, leaving rendered fat in the pot.
2. Add onion, green pepper, and carrots and cook for 5-10 minutes until onion is translucent.
3. Stir in tomatoes and tomato paste, seasonings, bay leaves, and Datil pepper or its alternative. Mix well.
4. Add reserved clam juice and fish stock, simmer on low heat for 1 hour.
5. Add potatoes and cook for an additional 20 minutes or until the potatoes are tender (not mushy). Add in the clams and cooked bacon, and continue cooking for another 5 minutes.

Potato Leek Soup

In my humble opinion leeks and potatoes are a match made in heaven, and this creamy soup is the proof. Simple yet elegant, it's suitable for all occasions- from a cozy night in on the couch to a fancy dinner party, it's always a crowd pleaser.

My kitchen tip: Over blending will result in a gluey texture instead of the velvety smoothness that we are looking for. If no immersion blender, a regular blender will work fine. Simply transfer the soup in batches and pulse lightly.

Ingredients:
- 3 Tbsp butter
- 3 cloves garlic, finely minced
- 3 leeks thinly sliced, dark green tops separated
- 2 lb. potatoes (russets work well), peeled and diced
- 6 cups chicken or vegetable broth
- 1 cup heavy cream
- salt & white pepper to taste

Directions:

1. Melt 2 Tbsp. butter in a heavy stockpot over medium heat, add garlic and leek whites and sauté until soft and translucent. Do not brown.
2. Add broth and potatoes, bring to a boil. Reduce heat, cover, and simmer gently for 25 minutes or until potatoes are very soft (almost falling apart).
3. Meanwhile, in a separate sauté pan, cook leek greens in remaining butter until soft and a bit crispy. Put to the side for garnish.
4. Remove from heat and lightly blend with an immersion blender JUST until smooth.
5. Season with salt and pepper, stir in ¾ of the cream.
6. Just before serving drizzle with a little more cream and top with the leek greens.

(Datil) Pumpkin Chili

This hearty stew offers a comforting blend of spice, balanced by the subtle sweetness of pumpkin. Here, pumpkin lends its creamy texture and mild flavor to make it a fantastic addition to your chili, deepening the taste and adding a touch of seasonal warmth. Give it a spicy kick by adding in cayenne or datil pepper dust for a bowl that will have you coming back for seconds.

Ingredients:
- 1 Tbsp olive oil or butter
- 1 yellow onion, diced
- 1 green bell pepper, diced
- 2 cloves garlic, minced
- 1 jalapeno, seeded and diced
- 1 ½ lb. ground beef or turkey
- 2 cups fresh pumpkin puree, or 1 15 oz. can
- 1 can kidney beans, drained and rinsed
- 1 can pinto beans, drained and rinsed
- 1 can black beans, drained and rinsed
- 1 can fire roasted diced tomatoes

- 1 can crushed tomatoes
- 6 oz can tomato paste
- 2 cups chicken broth
- 2 Tbsp chili powder
- 1 Tbsp cumin
- 2 tsp smoked paprika
- 2 tsp salt
- 1 tsp black pepper
- pinch of cayenne or datil pepper dust, optional

Directions:

1. Heat oil in a Dutch oven or large pot over medium-high heat, and sauté the onion, pepper, and jalapeno until soft and the onion is translucent. Add garlic and cook for an additional minute.
2. Add ground beef or turkey, and cook until browned and no pink remains, breaking it up as it cooks.
3. Reduce heat to medium low and stir in the pumpkin, beans, tomatoes and tomato paste, chicken broth, and all spices.
4. Cover and simmer for about 30 minutes, stirring occasionally.
5. After 30 minutes, taste and adjust seasoning as needed. Simmering longer if needed.

Autumn Harvest Salad with Blue Cheese Vinaigrette

This salad has it all- crispy, smoky, sweet and savory, and is extremely versatile. Don't have apples on hand? Switch it out for pears. Don't like apricots? Try mandarin oranges instead- the possibilities are endless. And it's all tied together with a tangy rich dressing. It's a delightful and elegant salad that's perfect for showcasing the season's bounty.

Ingredients:
- 4 cups spinach or mixed greens
- 4 oz crispy bacon pieces
- ½ medium apple, peeled and diced
- ¼ cup dried cranberries
- ¼ cup dried apricots, cut into small pieces
- ¼ cup pecan halves, roughly chopped and toasted
- ¼ cup blue cheese crumbles
- ¼ cup thinly sliced scallions

For the blue cheese Vinaigrette:
- 1 packet dry Italian dressing mix
- 1 tsp Dijon mustard
- 1 clove garlic, minced

- 2 Tbsp red wine vinegar
- 2 Tbsp balsamic vinegar
- ⅓ cup olive oil
- 3 Tbsp blue cheese crumbles
- salt & pepper to taste

Directions:

1. To make dressing- in a food processor or blender combine dry herb mix, mustard, garlic, and vinegars. Pulse to blend, then on low speed slowly drizzle in the olive oil until fully incorporated. Add the blue cheese crumbles and pulse a few more times to break up any large chunks of cheese.
2. Arrange the greens in a serving bowl and top with salad ingredients, drizzle with dressing before serving or tableside.

Brussel Sprout and Kale Salad with Citrus Vinaigrette

This vibrant and healthy salad combines the earthy goodness of shredded Brussels sprouts and kale with a bright, zesty citrus vinaigrette. It's a perfect side dish or a light and satisfying main.

My kitchen tip: Plan ahead- the Brussels sprouts and kale can be prepped and stored in an airtight container in the refrigerator for a day or two. The vinaigrette can also be made ahead of time. Dress the salad just before serving to prevent sogginess.

Ingredients:
- 1 lb. brussels sprouts, trimmed and thinly shredded
- 1 bunch kale, ribs removed and thinly sliced
- ½ cup dried cranberries or tart cherries
- ½ cup toasted pecans or walnuts, roughly chopped
- ¼ cup roasted chickpeas
- ¼ cup shaved Parmesan cheese

For the Citrus Vinaigrette:

- 2 Tbsp fresh orange juice
- 1 Tbsp fresh lemon juice
- 1 Tbsp white wine vinegar
- 1 tsp Dijon mustard
- ½ tsp honey
- ¼ cup extra virgin olive oil
- salt & pepper to taste

Directions:

1. Prepare the brussels sprouts and kale: If not already shredded, thinly slice the brussels sprouts using a mandoline or a sharp knife. For the kale, stack the destemmed leaves, roll them tightly, and slice them into thin ribbons. Place both in a large mixing bowl.
2. Make the Citrus Vinaigrette: In a small bowl or jar, whisk together the orange juice, lemon juice, white wine vinegar, honey, and Dijon mustard. Slowly drizzle in the olive oil while continuously whisking until the vinaigrette is emulsified and well combined. Season with salt and pepper to taste.
3. Assemble the Salad: Pour about half of the citrus vinaigrette over the shredded Brussels sprouts and kale. Using your hands, massage the dressing into the greens for 2-3 minutes. This step is crucial as it helps tenderize the Brussels sprouts and kale, making them more tender.
4. Add Remaining Ingredients: Add the dried cranberries, toasted nuts, and shaved parmesan to the bowl with the dressed greens.
5. Toss and Serve: Drizzle in more vinaigrette as needed, tossing gently to ensure all ingredients are

evenly coated. Taste and adjust seasoning if necessary. Serve immediately, or let it sit for 15-30 minutes for the flavors to meld.

Roasted Beet and Goat Cheese Salad

This salad combines the sweet earthiness of tender roasted beets with the tangy saltiness of crumbled goat cheese to create a refreshing and flavorful dish. Paired with a fruity balsamic vinaigrette, it makes a perfect light lunch or sophisticated side for any meal.

Ingredients:
- 5 beets, peeled and sliced wear gloves!
- 2 carrots, sliced
- olive oil
- salt & black pepper
- 4 oz goat cheese
- ¼ cup roasted walnuts
- arugula or spring mix
- 1 whole head of garlic, roasted
- ⅓ cup balsamic vinegar
- 1 Tbsp Dijon mustard
- 2 Tbsp honey

Directions:

1. Preheat oven to 400°
2. Place beets and carrots on a foil lined baking tray. Drizzle with olive oil and season with salt and pepper, tossing to coat. Roast for 30- 45 minutes or until veggies are tender.
3. Meanwhile, prepare roasted garlic. Keeping it whole and unpeeled, slice the top off of the garlic bulb to expose the cloves. Place it cut side up in aluminum foil, drizzle with olive oil, and season with salt. Loosely wrap and place into the oven with roasting vegetables. Once cooled, turn upside down and gently squeeze the bulbs from the bottom. The soft roasted cloves will slide right out.
4. While vegetables are cooling, prepare dressing by whisking together ½ cup of olive oil with roasted garlic, balsamic vinegar, Dijon mustard, honey, and salt/ pepper. Taste for seasoning and adjust as needed.
5. To assemble the salad place greens on serving dish and top with roasted vegetables, sprinkle with toasted walnuts and goat cheese, drizzle with dressing.

Citrus Salad with Feta and Mint

This citrus salad is a vibrant and refreshing dish, bursting with bright, tangy flavors. Use whatever citrus you prefer here, variety is the key. The citrus is beautifully complimented by the salty creaminess of the feta and the cool bite of fresh mint and onion, accented with the refreshing burst of vinaigrette.

Ingredients:
- 1 each blood orange, grapefruit, tangerine, and navel orange
- 4 oz feta cheese, crumbled
- 1 Tbsp fresh mint, chopped
- ¼ cup red onion finely sliced

For the dressing:
- ⅓ cup olive oil
- ¼ cup red wine vinegar
- ½ tsp Dijon mustard
- 1 garlic clove, minced
- Salt & pepper

Directions:

1. Prepare the dressing first- blend all ingredients and set aside for flavors to marry.
2. Slice off each end of the citrus, then standing the fruit on end, carefully cut down the side to remove the peel and white pith.
3. Turn the fruit on its side and sliced into wheels.
4. To prepare the salad, arrange the citrus on a plate or platter in an attractive tiled pattern. Sprinkle with mint, fetta, and onion, and drizzle with dressing.

Harvest Quinoa Salad

Bursting with fall flavors and colors, both sweet and savory all at once. This is no ordinary quinoa. It is a vibrant medley of roasted vegetables, crisp apples, and earthy goodness. It's a perfect hearty side or light meal that celebrates the best of autumn's bounty.

Ingredients:
- 1 cup uncooked quinoa, rinsed
- 1 cup butternut squash, peeled and cubed
- 1 apple, diced
- 1 green onion, thinly sliced
- 2 cups spinach, stems plucked and roughly torn
- ⅓ cup dried cranberries
- 2 Tbsp chopped pistachios
- 2 Tbsp toasted pepitas
- Salt & pepper

For the Cider Vinaigrette:
- 1 Tbsp Dijon mustard
- ⅓ cup of apple cider vinegar
- 1 Tbsp honey

- ⅓ cup olive oil
- 1 tsp orange zest
- salt & pepper

Directions:

1. Preheat oven to 400°
2. Roast butternut squash- place on a foil lined baking sheet and drizzle with olive oil. Sprinkle with salt and pepper. Toss to coat. Roast for approx. 30 minutes or until soft and cooked through. Set aside to cool.
3. While squash is cooking, prepare quinoa- In a medium saucepan, bring 2 cups of salted water to a boil. Add quinoa, reduce heat, cover, and cook for 15 minutes until all the water is absorbed.
4. Gently fluff with a fork and set cooked quinoa to the side to cool.
5. While squash and quinoa cool, prepare Cider Vinaigrette by whisking all ingredients together until thoroughly combined. The mixture will thicken and become creamier.
6. In a large bowl combine all components and toss gently with dressing, season with salt and pepper as needed. Refrigerate until ready to serve.

Part Four

Mains & Sides, The Heart of the Harvest Table

Inevitably our thoughts always turn to the centerpiece of the Autumn table- the main dish and its comforting companions, the sides. These recipes, passed down from generation to generation evoke fond memories of warmth and family with the first irresistible aromas. These are the stories we tell with food, passed down and savored with every last bite.

MY KITCHEN TIPS:

Plan ahead. Many recipes call for brines, marinades, and rubs which need to be done hours, even days ahead. When it's time for the show to begin, arrive early and take a moment to allow your ingredients to come to room temperature. This little bit of patience and planning ensures more even cooking and better development of flavors, resulting in a dish that showcases all your hard work.

Roasted Butternut Squash & Mushroom Lasagna

Discover layers of deliciousness in this celebration of seasonal flavors. This is the vegetarian dish that makes even the most devout carnivore smile. Each bite offers the sweet tenderness of roasted squash, the earthiness of sauteed mushrooms, and the creamy smoothness of a classic bechamel sauce, all nestled between layers of lovely pasta.

My kitchen tips: Lasagnas can be time-consuming and feel overwhelming, but they don't have to be. Broken down into its individual parts, it is much less daunting. There's nothing scary about roasted vegetables, sauce, noodles, and cheese! Plan and prepare ahead to make the task the enjoyable celebration of the season that it is intended to be.

Ingredients:
- 6 Tbsp unsalted butter, divided
- 2 ½ cups onions, diced
- 3 cups crimini mushrooms, sliced
- 1 butternut squash, peeled, seeded, and cut into 1/4-inch-thick slices (about 5 1/2 cups)

- 4 Tbsp fresh thyme, minced
- 4 Tbsp fresh sage leaves, minced
- ¼ cup all-purpose flour
- 4 cups whole milk
- Pinch of freshly grated nutmeg
- 1 ½ cups grated Fontina or Gruyere cheese
- 1 ½ cups grated Mozzarella cheese
- 1 ½ cups grated Parmesan cheese
- salt & pepper, as needed
- olive oil, as needed
- 19-ounce package no-boil lasagna noodles

Directions:

1. Preheat oven to 425°. Toss the squash with 1 Tbsp olive oil on a baking sheet and season with salt and pepper. Roast until squash is tender, about 15-20 minutes. Remove and set aside, reduce oven temperature to 350°.

2. While the squash is roasting, melt 4 Tbsp of the butter in a sauté pan over medium-high heat. Add onions and sauté until soft, about 8 minutes. Increase heat to high and add mushrooms, cook until tender, stirring constantly, about 3 minutes. Season with salt and pepper, remove and set aside.

3. Make the bechamel: In the sauté pan, melt the remaining 2 Tbsp of butter over medium heat. Add the sage and thyme and stir to coat, cooking for about a minute. Whisk in the flour until smooth. Continue to whisk and cook until the flour is lightly golden but not brown, about 2 minutes. Slowly whisk in the milk and bring to a gentle boil. Reduce heat and simmer until thickened, stirring occasionally, about 5 minutes. Stir in the nutmeg, salt and pepper to taste.

4. In a separate bowl, toss the cheeses together and season with salt and pepper.

5. Prepare a 9x13-inch glass or ceramic baking dish by brushing lightly with olive oil (or spray with pan spray if preferred).

6. Evenly coat the bottom of the dish with about ½ cup of the bechamel. Arrange 3 noodles side by side on top. Cover with ⅓ of the remaining bechamel. Sprinkle with ⅓ of the cheese mixture. Top with ½ each of the squash and mushroom mixtures. Lay 3 more noodles on top and repeat the layers (bechamel, cheese, squash, mushrooms). Top with the remaining 3 noodles, then cover with the remaining bechamel, and finally sprinkle with the last of the cheese.

7. Cover loosely with foil and bake until bubbly, about 35-45 minutes. Uncover and bake an additional 15- 25 minutes until top is browned and lasagna is heated through. Let stand 15 minutes before serving.

Citrus & Herb Roasted Turkey

As the centerpiece of the holiday table, this succulent turkey will not disappoint. It's infused with vibrant citrus and aromatic herbs, boasting a golden, crispy skin and juicy meat. Paired with a savory, herbaceous pan gravy and all the fixing the meal will be one to remember.

Ingredients
Citrus Rosemary salt:
- 1 Tbsp fresh rosemary leaves, chopped
- 2 Tbsp lemon zest
- 1/2 cup coarse salt

For the bird:
- One frozen turkey (average 12-16 lbs.), thawed in refrigerator
- 4 Tbsp (more or less, depending on size of the turkey) unsalted butter, softened and cut into small pieces
- 4 sprigs fresh rosemary
- 4 sprigs fresh thyme
- ½ bunch fresh parsley stems, reserving the leaves for other purposes

- 2 bay leaves
- 4 cloves garlic
- 2 lemons, quartered
- 1 sweet or yellow onion, peeled and quartered
- four large carrots, peeled and halved lengthwise
- eight celery stalks

For the gravy:

- 2 sweet or yellow onions, peeled and quartered
- 2 carrots, peeled and cut into large pieces
- 2 celery stalks, cut into large pieces
- 1 bay leaf
- ½ bunch of parsley stems
- 2 qt (8 cups) chicken broth or stock, divided
- 8 Tbsp unsalted butter (one stick)
- ½ cup all-purpose flour
- salt and pepper to taste

Directions:

1. To make the citrus Rosemary salt combine all three ingredients in a food processor and pulse until well blended. Remove to a bowl and set aside.
2. Adjust oven rack to its lowest position and remove the other racks. Preheat the oven to 500°F. Arrange the halved carrots and celery stalks in the center of a roasting pan and put to the side in preparation for the turkey.
3. Remove the neck and giblets from the turkey and set them aside. Pat the turkey dry with paper towels both inside and out. Carefully slide your fingers or the handle of a spoon under the skin of the turkey breast, working from the neck cavity

down towards the legs. Be gentle to avoid tearing the skin. Once loosened, insert most of the small pieces of softened butter under the skin, extending over the entire breast and down towards the leg joints. Gently massage the skin from the outside to help distribute the butter evenly. With the rest of the butter, coat the outside of the skin and sprinkle liberally with the citrus rosemary salt.

4. Stuff the herbs, garlic, lemon, and onion inside the cavity. It doesn't have to be perfect, it's fine if some of it falls out. Place the bird on top of the prepared carrots and celery in the roasting pan and tuck the wings under.

5. Roast for 30 minutes. Remove from the oven and cover lightly with aluminum foil. Return to the oven and reduce oven temperature to 350°F. Cook for approx. 2- ½ hours, until a thermometer inserted into the thickest part of the breast and/ or thigh reads 165°. Remove from the oven and let rest. Remove and discard onion, lemon, herbs, etc. from the turkey cavity before serving. Use any pan drippings in the gravy.

6. While the turkey roasts, place the neck and giblets into a large saucepan. Add ½ of the broth, onions, carrots, celery, and herbs (you can include any leftover bits or pieces of herbs not used in the turkey). Bring to a boil over high heat and then reduce the heat to medium and simmer until reduced by about ½. Strain and discard vegetables. Set the broth aside, this will be the base of your gravy.

7. While the turkey rests, finish the gravy. In a saucepan, melt butter and add flour. Whisk over

medium heat for 3-4 minutes, or until a smooth, blonde- colored mixture is formed (this is called a Roux). Add the reserved turkey stock and any pan juices and bring to a boil. Reduce the heat and simmer until thickened and ready to serve. Season with salt and pepper to taste.

Pot Roast with Autumn Vegetables

Fork tender beef is slow cooked to perfection in a rich sauce with hearty seasonal herbs and vegetables to create a meal that is both comforting and satisfying. Serve with warm rosemary honey rolls to sopp up any leftover sauce.

Ingredients:
- 3 ½ - 4-pound boneless beef chuck roast
- salt and pepper, as needed
- ¼ cup vegetable or canola oil
- ½ cup all-purpose flour
- 8 small, red-skinned potatoes, halved
- 2 carrots, peeled and cut into large chunks
- 1 ½ cup butternut squash, peeled and cut into large chunks
- 1 red onion, peeled and cut into large chunks
- 2 Tbsp tomato paste
- 5 cloves garlic, peeled and smashed
- 3 sprigs fresh thyme
- 1 Tbsp rosemary leaves, minced
- 1 tsp. dried oregano

- 2 bay leaves
- Two 12-ounce bottles stout beer (like Guiness)
- 2 ½ cups beef stock
- 1 ½ Tbsp cornstarch dissolved in 3 Tbsp water

Directions:

1. The night before, season the chuck roast liberally with salt and pepper and refrigerate uncovered. When ready to cook, preheat the oven to 300°.
2. In a large Dutch oven or stock pot, heat the oil over medium-high heat. Season the roast again with salt and pepper and dust with flour, shaking off the excess. Sear on all sides, browning the meat evenly, about 4- 6 minutes per side. Remove the roast from the pot and set aside.
3. Add the carrots, squash, and onion to the pot, reduce the heat to medium and cook, stirring occasionally, until the vegetables are caramelized, about 6- 8 minutes. Stir in the tomato paste, garlic, and herbs and cook for another 2 minutes.
4. Add the roast back to the pot, then add the beer, beef stock, and potatoes. Nestle the roast down among the vegetables so that it is mostly submerged in the liquid. Bring to a simmer.
5. Cover, leaving the lid slightly ajar, and place in the oven to cook until tender, about 3- 3 ½ hours, testing for tenderness at 3 hours.
6. Once done, remove the roast and vegetables from the pot. Discard the thyme and bay leaves.
7. To thicken the sauce, place pot back on the stove and bring to a simmer over medium-high heat. Simmer, stirring occasionally, until the liquid is reduced slightly. Slowly whisk in part of the

cornstarch mixture and continue to simmer for 1 minute. Add more of the cornstarch mixture if needed to reach the desired thickness. You may not need the cornstarch at all- remember that it will cause the sauce to continue to thicken as it cools. You're looking for a rich and smooth sauce overall.

8. Carve pot roast into thick slices and serve with vegetables and sauce.

Cider Braised Pork Tenderloin with Apples

Experience the comforting flavors of fall with this tender pork-slow braised to perfection in a rich, tangy cider reduction and juicy baked apples. Add in fresh herb and garlic and you manage to turn the ordinary into extraordinary, perfect for a cozy night in or wowing your guests.

My kitchen tips: This is the perfect recipe to show off your homemade apple cider, good thing you made extra!

Ingredients:
- 1 pork tenderloin, 1-½ pounds
- 1 tsp salt
- ½ tsp ground black pepper
- 3 sprigs of fresh thyme
- 1 Tbsp olive oil
- 2 garlic cloves, minced
- 1 shallot, minced
- ½ sweet or yellow onion, diced
- 1 cup fresh apple cider
- 1 Tbsp fresh rosemary, finely chopped

- 1 Tbsp fresh thyme, finely chopped
- 2 Tbsp Dijon mustard
- 2 apples, cored and sliced; tart apples like granny smith work best
- 1 Tbsp butter
- salt and pepper, to taste

Directions:

1. Place the salt, pepper, and thyme in the bowl of a mortar and pestle and grind together. You can also use a small food processor or blender.
2. Pat the pork dry with a paper towel and rub the herb mixture into the pork. Wrap in plastic wrap and put in the refrigerator overnight or for at least 3 hours.
3. Preheat the oven to 350°
4. When ready to cook, rinse the salt/ herb mixture off the pork and pat dry. Add the oil to the bottom of a heavy-bottomed stock pot or Dutch oven and sear on all sides over medium-high heat. Transfer the pork to a plate lined with paper towels to absorb any excess oil.
5. Add the shallots, onion, and garlic and sauté for 1-2 minutes. Add the cider, scraping the bottom to remove any browning bits.
6. Add the rosemary, thyme and mustard to the skillet, increase the heat and bring the mixture to a boil, stirring often. Return the pork to the pan, cover and transfer to the oven and cook for 20 minutes.
7. Remove from the oven and add the apple slices and continue to cook, covered, in the oven for an additional 15-20 minutes until the apples are

slightly soft but still firm and the pork registers 145° on a meat thermometer.

8. If the pork is fully cooked and your apples are not as soft as you would like, remove the pork from the pan and let the apples continue to bake until they are done.

9. Transfer the apples and pork to a plate and allow to rest before carving.

10. While the pork is resting, strain the cooking liquid, place the pot over medium-high heat and bring the liquid to a boil. If you prefer extra sauce, you can add more cider. Simmer and allow it to reduce by ⅓, remove from heat and whisk in the butter to make a glossy sauce. Season with salt and pepper and transfer the sauce to a serving dish.

Orange Glazed Salmon

This is a recipe that I started making when cooking for a small neighborhood golf club that has evolved a lot throughout the years. It was popular then, and it's still one of my personal favorite ways to make salmon. it's incredibly flavorful, with a perfect balance of sweet, savory, and tangy notes, and enhanced with the subtle nutty aroma of sesame. And I love that the marinade does double duty, infusing the salmon with incredible flavors before being reduced into a luscious glaze.

Ingredients

For the Marinade & Glaze:

- Juice of 1 orange, about ¼ cup
- zest of one orange, about 1 Tbsp
- 2 Tbsp orange marmalade
- 2 Tbsp low-sodium soy sauce
- 2 Tbsp brown sugar
- 1 Tbsp grated fresh ginger
- 2 cloves garlic, minced
- 1 tsp rice vinegar
- ½ cup chicken or vegetable broth

- ½ tsp toasted sesame oil
- 1 tsp cornstarch, optional, for thicker glaze
- 1 Tbsp cold water, if using cornstarch
- 1 Tbsp unsalted butter, cold and cut into small pieces

For the Salmon:
- 2 (6-8 oz) salmon fillets, skin on or off
- 1 Tbsp. olive oil
- salt and freshly ground black pepper to taste
- orange slices and sesame seed for garnish

Directions:

1. In a medium bowl, whisk together the orange juice, zest, and marmalade, along with the soy sauce, brown sugar, ginger, garlic, and rice vinegar. This is your marinade.
2. Place the salmon fillets in a shallow dish or a resealable bag. Pour about half of the marinade over the salmon, ensuring it's well-coated. Reserve the remainder of the marinade for the glaze.
3. Marinate the salmon in the refrigerator for 20-30 minutes. Don't marinate for too long (over 30 minutes), especially if using thinner fillets, as the acidity in the orange juice can start to "cook" the fish.
4. While the salmon is marinating, pour the reserved marinade into a small saucepan with the chicken or vegetable broth.
5. If you prefer a thicker glaze, whisk together the cornstarch and cold water in a small bowl until smooth.
6. Bring the mixture to a simmer over medium heat. If using, slowly whisk in the cornstarch slurry. Continue to simmer, stirring occasionally, for 7-10

minutes, or until the glaze has reduced and thickened to your desired consistency. It should be syrupy enough to coat the back of a spoon. Remove from heat and stir in the toasted sesame oil. Then, gradually whisk in the cold butter, one piece at a time, until it's fully incorporated and the glaze is glossy. Do not return to a boil after adding the butter. Set aside.

7. Preheat your oven to 400°

8. Remove the salmon from the marinade and pat the fillets dry with paper towels. Season both sides lightly with salt and pepper. Discard the used marinade.

9. Put the oil into an oven-safe sauté pan over medium high heat. Once shimmering, carefully place the salmon fillets skin-side down (if applicable). Sear for 3-4 minutes until the skin is crispy and golden brown.

10. Transfer the sauté pan to the oven. (If you do not have an oven safe pan, carefully transfer the salmon to a baking dish)

11. Brush the salmon fillets generously with the prepared orange glaze.

12. Bake for 8-12 minutes, or until the salmon is cooked through and flakes easily with a fork. The cooking time will vary depending on the thickness of your fillets.

13. Carefully transfer the salmon to serving plates. Drizzle with any remaining glaze from the pan. Garnish with a fresh orange slice and a sprinkle of sesame seeds, if desired.

Mashed Potatoes

In our family, creamy homemade mashed potatoes are a staple at every holiday meal and quite frequently in between. It's just one of those comfort foods that everyone loves. This makes a lot of potatoes, but I can guarantee that no one will be complaining about the leftovers. The recipe is easy to scale down for less people- estimate one potato per person plus one or two more for good measure (depending on size), and reduce the amount of cream cheese, etc. accordingly.

My kitchen tips: I find that a stand mixer whips the potatoes more efficiently without overworking them, keeping the texture lighter and fluffier instead of heavy and gluey.

Ingredients:
- 5 lb. bag of russet potatoes, peeled and quartered
- 3-4 whole garlic cloves, peeled
- 1 8 oz package cream cheese, softened to room temperature
- 4-8 Tbsp (1-½ stick) unsalted butter, softened to room temperature + more as desired

- chicken broth as needed, up to 2 cups (You will most likely not need that much unless you prefer thinner potatoes)
- ½ cup sour cream, optional
- salt and pepper, to taste
- chopped fresh chives for garnish

Directions:

1. Place prepared potatoes and garlic in a large heavy stock pot filled with cold salted water.
2. Bring to a gentle boil and cook until potatoes are fork tender. A fork inserted into a potato should pierce it easily, but it should not break or fall apart.
3. Strain the water from the potatoes and garlic and transfer them to the bowl of a stand mixer fitted with a whisk attachment. If you prefer to mash by hand, then return to the stock pot.
4. Add cream cheese, ½ of the stick of butter, ½ cup of broth, sour cream if desired, and a generous dash of salt and pepper. Whip/mash enough to start breaking up the potato pieces and mixing ingredients.
5. Add more broth and whip again to incorporate, tasting for seasoning and butter as you go.
6. You may need to repeat a few times to reach desired consistency- but remember not to over whip into that gluey texture.
7. Top with chopped chives.

Bourbon Bacon Brussel Sprouts

You will delight in these perfectly tender- crisp roasted brussel sprouts. Elevated with nuggets of savory, crumbled bacon and coated in a delectably sweet and smoky bourbon reduction, this simple side dish is sure to impress.

Ingredients:

- 2-4 slices thick-cut applewood bacon, cut into 1inch pieces
- 2 cloves garlic, minced
- 1 lb. brussels sprouts, trimmed and quartered
- ½ tsp each salt, smoked paprika, and freshly ground black pepper
- ¼ cup brown sugar, packed
- 1 Tbsp bourbon

Directions:

1. In a large sauté pan over medium heat, cook bacon until crispy. With a slotted spoon remove the bacon to a paper towel covered plate or dish.

2. Pour off all but 4 Tbsp bacon fat from the sauté pan.
3. Return sauté pan to the heat. Add garlic and brussel sprouts cut-side down. Let cook, undisturbed, until bottoms are golden and edges are crispy, 5- 6 minutes. Add salt, paprika, and pepper, and continue to cook, stirring occasionally, until sprouts are golden all over and tender, 4- 5 more minutes.
4. Stir in brown sugar and bourbon, and cook until thick and syrupy, about 2- 3 minutes. Return bacon to skillet and toss to coat.
5. Sprinkle with more salt, pepper, and paprika to taste and serve warm.

Cheesy Cabbage Gratin

This beautiful gratin transforms the humblest of vegetables into a remarkably comforting and flavorful side. Tender, slow cooked cabbage is baked in a rich, creamy cheese sauce until bubbling and golden, making it an irresistible addition to any meal.

My kitchen tip: The gratin can be baked a day ahead without the final step. Keep chilled in the refrigerator until ready to finish and serve. Bring to room temperature, sprinkle with Gruyere and topping and broil.

Ingredients:
- 1 medium head of cabbage, cut into 8 wedges and each wedge cut in half
- olive oil, as needed
- salt and pepper, plus more as needed
- 1 shallot, thinly sliced
- 3 cloves garlic, thinly sliced
- 1 ½ cup heavy cream
- 1 Tbsp fresh thyme, plus more for garnish

- 1 tsp crushed red pepper flake, adjust as necessary to suit your taste
- 1 cup Parmesan, finely grated, divided
- ½ cup Gruyère cheese, grated
- 2 Tbsp unsalted butter, melted
- ½ cup panko breadcrumbs

Directions:

1. Preheat oven to 350° Coat the inside of a 3-qt. shallow baking dish with butter or cooking spray.
2. Place cabbage cut side down on a rimmed baking sheet, drizzle with oil and season lightly with salt and pepper. Roast until tender and edges are golden, 40–45 minutes, flipping them ½ way through. This is an essential first step not only for both caramelization and flavor development, but also to draw out moisture and keep the final product from becoming watery.
3. Meanwhile, in a small saucepan over medium heat sauté shallots and garlic in a small amount of butter for 2-3 minutes. Reduce heat to low and add cream, thyme, 1½ tsp salt, and red pepper flake. Bring to a simmer and cook, stirring occasionally, until shallots and garlic are very soft, about 15 minutes. Let cool slightly and use an immersion blender (or transfer to a countertop blender) to blend until smooth. Whisk in ½ cup parmesan until melted.
4. Arrange roasted cabbage in the baking dish and pour cream mixture over. Bake on middle rack until cream thickens, 30–40 minutes, covering with foil halfway through. Let cool slightly.

5. While the gratin is baking, combine melted butter, panko breadcrumbs, and remaining ½ cup of parmesan. Set aside.

6. Increase oven temperature to broil. Sprinkle Gruyère and Parmesan topping evenly over cabbage. Broil until cheese is bubbling and the top is browning in spots, about 4-6 minutes. Garnish with fresh thyme.

Orange Kissed Cranberry Sauce

I've said it before and I'll say it again, I love cranberries. I put them in drinks, on salads, and in all kinds of dishes. Unlike the store-bought stuff, this homemade sauce is not too sweet and utterly delicious. Make double the recipe and use for cranberry sauce muffins or cranberry bars.

My kitchen tip: Don't forget that cranberries float! You don't want to accidentally add too much liquid; it will take much longer for the sauce to reduce and you run the risk of the berries becoming bitter. (not that I'm saying this from experience or anything...)

Ingredients:
- 2 (12 oz) packages fresh cranberries
- 2 cups (1 pint) orange juice
- Zest of 1 orange
- 1 ½- 2 cups dark brown sugar, packed, depending on preferred sweetness level
- 1 Tbsp ground cinnamon

Directions:

1. Rinse the cranberries under cold water, picking out any soft, shriveled, or bruised berries.
2. Combine all the ingredients in a medium saucepan and bring to a boil over high heat.
3. Reduce heat and simmer gently, stirring occasionally. As the berries cook, they will begin to pop and the sauce will start to thicken, this is a good time to taste and add more sugar if needed. You can also gently mash some of the berries with the back of your spoon against the side of the pot. Continue cooking a little bit more until it has reached your desired thickness. Overall, they will cook for anywhere between 15- 30 minutes.
4. If you prefer a chunkier sauce, cook for less time and remove once the sauce has thickened but the berries are still there. If you prefer a smoother sauce, cook for more time to allow the berries to break down completely, you can also puree with an immersion blender. The longer it cooks, the thicker it will be.

Herbed Brown Butter Green Beans with Toasted Pecans

Elevate your classic green bean side dish with the rich, warm flavors of autumn. Here we've transformed simple green beans into a sophisticated culinary experience (and it's not even hard!). With the aromatic depth of herbs and the nutty richness of brown butter and pecans, it's perfect for your holiday table or any fall gathering. This dish is a testament to how simple quality ingredients can create something truly extraordinary.

Ingredients:
- 1 lb. fresh green beans, trimmed
- ½ cup pecan halves
- 8 Tbsp (1 stick) unsalted butter, cut into pieces
- 20-25 fresh sage leaves (some for butter, some for crispy garnish)
- 2 sprigs fresh thyme
- 1 small sprig fresh rosemary
- 1 large shallot, finely minced
- 1-2 tsp lemon juice
- Salt & pepper, to taste

Directions:

1. Bring a pot of salted water to a boil. Add the trimmed green beans and blanch for 3-5 minutes, or until bright green and crisp-tender. Immediately drain and plunge into an ice bath to stop the cooking and preserve their vibrant color. Drain very well and set aside.
2. In a dry sauté pan over medium heat, toast the pecan halves until fragrant and lightly browned, about 3-5 minutes, be careful not to burn them. Remove from sauté pan and set aside.
3. Wipe out the pan if needed. Add the butter, and over medium heat let it melt and begin to brown, stirring occasionally. Once it starts to turn a nutty brown and smells fragrant, add the minced shallot, about 15-20 sage leaves, the thyme sprigs, and the rosemary sprig.
4. Continue to cook for 1-2 minutes until the shallots are translucent and the sage leaves are crispy.
5. Carefully remove the crispy sage leaves with tongs and set aside on a paper towel to crumble over the dish later. Discard the thyme and rosemary sprigs, as their flavor has been infused.
6. Add the blanched green beans and toasted pecans to the skillet with the shallot brown butter. Toss gently to coat everything and warm through for 2-3 minutes.
7. Remove from heat and stir in the fresh lemon juice to brighten the flavors. Season generously with salt and pepper to taste.

8. Transfer the green beans to a serving dish. Crumble the reserved crispy sage leaves over the top. Finish with a sprinkle of flaky sea salt if desired for extra texture and flavor. Serve immediately.

Collard Greens with Smoky Bacon

Collard greens are a true Southern staple, and let's be honest, they spark strong opinions—you either love them, or you don't! If you're a fan, or curious to become one, this recipe is for you. We're talking tender greens infused with smoky thick-cut bacon, savory onion and garlic, and balanced with a touch of sweet, a touch of tang, and a kick of heat. Get ready for a dish that might just convert you.

My kitchen tips: Using pre-washed and cut collards significantly reduces prep time, getting this soulful side dish on your table that much faster.

Make Ahead: Collard greens often taste even better the next day, as the flavors have more time to meld. Reheat gently on the stovetop or in the microwave.

Don't Rush It: The key to tender, flavorful collard greens is a long, slow simmer. Don't try to rush the cooking process.

Ingredients:
- one package thick cut smoked bacon, diced into 1/2-inch pieces

- 2 (16-ounce) bags pre-washed and cut collard greens, about 2 lb. total
- 1 ½ yellow onions, diced
- 4-5 cloves garlic, minced
- 1 tsp red pepper flakes (or more, to taste, if you like more heat)
- ⅓ cup apple cider vinegar
- 2 Tbsp sugar
- 1 Tbsp Worcestershire sauce
- 3 Tbsp roasted chicken bouillon paste (I like Better than Bouillon brand)
- enough water to cover, approximately 10 cups
- salt and pepper, to taste

Directions:

1. Place the diced bacon in a large Dutch oven or stock pot. Cook over medium heat, stirring occasionally, until the bacon is crispy and has rendered most of its fat. This will take about 10-15 minutes.
2. Using a slotted spoon, remove the crispy bacon from the pot and set it aside on a paper towel-lined plate. Leave the rendered bacon fat in the pot.
3. Add the onion to the pot and cook over medium heat, stirring occasionally, until softened and translucent, about 5-7 minutes.
4. Add the minced garlic and red pepper flakes to the pot and cook for another 1-2 minutes until fragrant, being careful not to burn the garlic.
5. Add the collard greens to the pot in batches. Using tongs, toss and stir the greens with the rendered bacon fat, onion, garlic, and red pepper flakes until all the greens are coated and slightly wilted down.

It will seem like a lot at first, but they will cook down significantly.

6. Pour in the apple cider vinegar, scraping the bottom of the pot with a wooden or silicone spoon to loosen any browned bits. Cook for 1 minute until the vinegar has slightly reduced.

7. Stir in the Worcestershire sauce, sugar, bouillon and water. Stir well to combine all ingredients.

8. Bring the mixture to a gentle simmer and cook for several hours, until the greens are very tender. The longer they cook, the more tender and flavorful they will become. Stir occasionally to ensure even cooking.

9. Once the collard greens are tender, taste and adjust seasoning with salt and freshly ground black pepper as needed. Stir in most of the reserved crispy bacon, reserving some for garnish if desired.

Sausage & Herb Dressing

Every year, as the holidays approach, this is one dish I absolutely must make. It's my favorite go-to, a guaranteed crowd-pleaser that brings incredible flavor and a comforting aroma to any festive table. There's just something about the earthiness of the herbs that perfectly complements the savory sausage, that creates a harmonious blend that's simply irresistible. This recipe is a tradition for a reason – it's truly the best.

Ingredients:
- 1 lb. country sausage (mild or sage)
- 2 cups onion, diced
- 1 cup celery, diced
- 2 tsp rubbed sage
- 1 tsp marjoram
- ⅓ cup fresh parsley, chopped
- 2 cups +/- low sodium chicken broth
- salt & pepper, to taste
- 10 cups dry bread cubes
- 2 Tbsp unsalted butter, cut into small pieces

Directions:

1. Preheat oven to 350°
2. Cook sausage in a large sauté pan over medium-high heat until browned. Remove with a slotted spoon and place on a paper towel lined plate to drain.
3. In the pan dripping, cook onions and celery until onion is translucent and beginning to brown, and celery is tender. Add to the sausage.
4. In a very large mixing bowl, mix the sausage, onion/ celery mixture and herbs. Add the bread cubes and mix to incorporate.
5. Drizzle chicken broth over top ½ cup at a time, tossing in between each addition, to evenly moisten the bread cubes. You do not want them to be fully soggy as you do this, unless you prefer your end result to be a wetter dressing. Season with salt and pepper to taste.
6. Spread mixture evenly into a 9x 13-inch baking dish and dot top with butter.
7. Cover and bake for about 30-40 minutes, until fully warmed through. Uncover and bake an addition 10 minutes until browned.

Sunrise Apple-Cranberry Dressing

Get ready to brighten your holiday table with this vibrant dressing. It's a delightful medley of sweet apples and tender dried fruits that will add a burst of flavor and color to your feast. It's the perfect sweet and savory side compliment to your meal.

My kitchen tip: if you don't prefer apricots or cranberries, switch them out for other dried fruits like cherries and raisins.

You can use any type of bread that you enjoy, making it uniquely your own. Sourdough would be an amazing compliment to the fruits here.

Ingredients:
- 6 Tbsp unsalted butter
- 1 lb. sliced country white bread
- 1 large cooking apple, cored and diced
- 1 medium onion, diced
- 2 celery ribs with leaves, diced
- ½ cup dried apricots, roughly chopped

- ⅓ cup fresh parsley, chopped
- ¼ cup dried cranberries
- 2-3 sprigs fresh thyme, chopped
- salt and pepper to taste
- pinch fennel seed, optional
- 3 cups chicken broth
- 1 large egg, beaten
- 2 Tbsp melted butter

Directions:

1. Preheat oven to 325°, grease a 9x13 casserole dish.
2. Cut or tear bread into bite-size pieces and lay out in a single layer on 1- 2 baking sheets. Toast until slightly dry and crispy, about 15 to 20 minutes. Set aside to cool.
3. Melt 6 Tbsp of butter in a large sauté pan over medium high heat. Add the fruits, onion, celery and herbs; season with salt and pepper and cook until soft, about 5 minutes.
4. Add the broth and bring to a boil, remove from heat.
5. In a large bowl mix together the egg, toasted bread, onion and fruit mixture and parsley, and toss until evenly moistened. Loosely pack the dressing into the prepared pan.
6. Bake uncovered, about 40 minutes. Drizzle the melted butter over the top and cook approximately 20 more minutes until top is crisp and golden.

Lemon Rice with Asparagus & Peas

Brighten up your plate with this fresh and vibrant dish that's so simple yet so flavorful. It brings together the brightness of lemon, the crisp tenderness of fresh asparagus, and the sweet pop of peas beautifully, for a wonderfully light and refreshing addition to any meal.

Ingredients:
- 1 Tbsp olive oil
- ½ cup yellow onion, diced
- 1 ½ cups long grained white rice
- 3 cups water
- 1 Tbsp chicken bouillon paste
- 2 Tbsp unsalted butter
- 1 lemon slice
- 1 tsp grated lemon zest, plus more for garnish
- 1 lb. fresh asparagus
- 1 ½ cups fresh or frozen peas
- salt and pepper, to taste
- 1 cup parmesan cheese, freshly grated or shaved

Directions:

1. Heat the olive oil in a medium saucepan; add the onion and cook until softened, about 4 minutes. Add the rice and toast the grains, stirring occasionally, until the rice begins to look opaque/bright white, about 4 minutes. Add the water, bouillon, butter, lemon slice and zest, cover and reduce the heat to low; simmer for 25 minutes.

2. While the rice is cooking, prepare and cook the asparagus and peas. For the asparagus: Break off the tough ends of the asparagus stalks and discard. Cut the spears on the diagonal into 1-inch lengths. Place a steamer rack into a pot with about ½ inch of water and bring to a simmer. Steam the asparagus to cook just until tender, about 4-5 minutes.

3. For the peas: Boil in salted water for 3-4 minutes till just done. Rinse under cold water to stop the cooking and preserve green color.

4. Remove the lemon slice from the cooked rice and discard. Transfer rice to a serving bowl. Season with salt and pepper and toss in asparagus and peas. Sprinkle with additional lemon zest and fresh parmesan just before serving.

Autumn Root Vegetables with Orange Glaze

This dish was inspired by one that I found on the internet while looking for a different take on sweet potatoes that didn't involve marshmallows and was a bit healthier. This vibrant gratin features thinly sliced sweet potatoes, carrots, and parsnips baked in a fragrant orange-maple glaze that's been infused with fresh herbs and finished with a scattering of bright pomegranate arils. It's a beautiful and flavorful side dish, perfect for holiday gatherings, offering a healthier twist on classic casseroles.

My kitchen tips: Cannot find or don't like parsnips or carrots? It's an easy adjustment to remove one or the other. Simply increase to 3 sweet potatoes (about 2 ½ lbs.) and 4-5 carrots or parsnips (about 1 ½ lbs.)

Ingredients:
- 2 large sweet potatoes (about 2 lbs.), peeled
- 3-4 medium carrots (about 1 lb.), peeled
- 3-4 medium parsnips (about 1 lb.), peeled
- 1 ½ Tbsp unsalted butter, melted

- zest and juice of 1 orange (about ½ cup juice)
- 6 Tbsp Pure Maple Syrup, NOT pancake syrup
- 1 ½ tsp vanilla
- ¾ tsp salt
- 1 Tbsp fresh thyme leaves, finely chopped
- 1 Tbsp. fresh rosemary, finely chopped
- ¾ tsp. ground cinnamon
- ½ tsp ground allspice
- ⅛ tsp ground ginger
- 3 Tbsp unsweetened pomegranate juice, chilled
- 2 tsp cornstarch
- ½ cup pomegranate arils, for garnish

Directions:

1. Preheat your oven to 375°. Lightly grease a 9x13-inch baking dish with 1/2 Tbsp of the melted butter
2. Using a mandoline slicer or a sharp knife, carefully slice the sweet potatoes, carrots, and parsnips into uniform ⅛- ¼ inch thick rounds. Even thickness is key for consistent cooking.
3. Arrange the sliced vegetables in the prepared baking dish, tiling and alternating the vegetables for an appealing presentation.
4. In a medium bowl, whisk together the orange juice and zest, maple syrup, vanilla, salt, herbs, and spices. In a separate small bowl, dissolve the cornstarch into the chilled pomegranate juice to create a slurry. Add this slurry to the orange juice mixture and whisk until everything is well combined.

5. Pour the prepared glaze evenly over the arranged vegetables and drizzle the remaining melted butter over the top.

6. Bake for about 50 minutes, or until the vegetables are tender when pierced with a fork and the glaze has thickened and is bubbling. If the top begins to brown too quickly, you can loosely tent the dish with aluminum foil.

7. Just before serving, sprinkle generously with fresh pomegranate arils.

Part Five

Desserts & Sweet Endings

There's no more perfect way to conclude a cozy meal than with a sweet embrace. For me, desserts are where the magic truly unfolds- taking all that the season has to offer and creating comforting, heartwarming treats. That sweet fragrance whispers of family gathering long after the meal is done- creating sweet memories, cherished moments, and the promise of more to come.

MY KITCHEN TIPS:

While cooking invites a dash of creativity and a pinch of intuition, when it comes to baking your recipe is a trusted friend who is there to make sure that your chemistry experiment doesn't explode! Take a moment to read through all the steps before you begin. Follow the directions carefully, being sure to pay attention to measurements and temperatures. This will ensure those delightful textures and lovely flavors that you were hoping for, with none of the guesswork and all the delicious success.

A word about vanilla- It's a divine flavor that is used in just about every baking recipe and more, but the good stuff can be expensive. You'll notice that I favor vanilla bean paste, as it gives you a pure vanilla bean flavor with all the little specs of vanilla bean seeds, but without the extra work of scraping seeds from the bean pods or the extra cost. You can usually find it at most specialty or premium grocery stores, but you can substitute vanilla extract equally in any of my recipes. If you do choose to purchase whole vanilla beans don't throw them out after scraping the seeds!! There are so many uses for these lovely little seed pods that I can't even begin to go into. You'll never think of vanilla as plain or simple again.

Maple Pecan Tartlets

Pecan trees are everywhere in Florida, and you can find these amazing nuts in everything during the fall. Perfect topped with a scoop of creamy vanilla ice cream, these sumptuous little versions of pecan pie are the perfect ending to any fall meal, and best of all, you don't have to share!

Ingredients:
- 24 store bought mini tart shells, uncooked *
- ⅓ cup unsalted butter, melted
- 5 Tbsp good quality pure maple syrup (NOT pancake syrup)
- 1 ½ cups dark brown sugar, packed
- 2 eggs
- 1 cup pecan halves, rough chopped

Directions:

1. Preheat the oven to 350°
2. In a medium mixing bowl combine melted butter,

maple syrup, brown sugar, and eggs. Mix well, then stir in pecans.

3. Arrange tart shells on a baking sheet and fill approx. ¾ of the way full of the filling.
4. Bake for 20-25 minutes, until pastry edges are golden brown and filling is set.
5. Cool completely before serving.

*If you prefer to make your own tart shells, try the simple flaky pie crust to follow.

Seminole Pumpkin Pie

Who knew that Florida has its own native variety of heat tolerant pumpkin? It's called the Seminole pumpkin, and it has a sweeter flavor than the traditional grocery store pumpkin, with a pale outer skin and beautiful bright orange flesh. Surely Bithia and Cordelia had this lovely fruit on their autumn tables as both decor and part of the meal!!

In this recipe we are using fresh Seminole pumpkin puree, but canned pumpkin can be substituted equally.

MY KITCHEN TIP:

In this recipe we are using fresh Seminole pumpkin puree, but normal pie pumpkins can be used to make your fresh puree too. Canned pumpkin can be substituted equally in the recipe as well.

Ingredients:
- pie crust, store bought or homemade, recipe to follow
- 2 cups Seminole pumpkin puree, recipe to follow
- 3 large eggs

- 1 ¼ cups dark brown sugar, packed
- 1 Tbsp cornstarch
- ½ tsp. salt
- 1 ½ tsp cinnamon
- ½ tsp ground ginger
- ¼ tsp grated nutmeg
- ⅛ tsp ground cloves
- 18 tsp ground black pepper
- 1 cup heavy cream
- ¼ cup milk

Directions:

1. Preheat oven to 375°
2. If using homemade, prepare the pie crust- recipe below. Cover center of crust with parchment paper and add pie weights, par-bake for 10 minutes and remove parchment/ weights.
3. To make the filling whisk the pumpkin puree, eggs, and brown sugar together until combined. Add the cornstarch, spices, cream, and milk. Whisk vigorously until everything is combined.
4. Pour the pie filling into the warm par-baked crust. Only fill about ¾ of the way full, there may be extra. (perfect for mini pies with leftover dough scraps!)
5. Bake for 50-60 minutes, until the center is almost set. About ½ way through cooking, cover the edges of the crust with a pie shield or aluminum foil to prevent it from becoming too brown.
6. Once done, transfer to a wire rack to cool completely before serving.

SEMINOLE PUMPKIN PUREE

I highly recommend doubling or tripling the batch for use in all your other delectable recipes, from chili and scones to martinis, there are so many amazing uses for a great pumpkin puree. Each pound of pumpkin makes about ¾ of a cup of puree. This method can be used for any variety of pumpkin or other hard squash and can be stored in the refrigerator in an airtight container for up to a week, or portioned out and frozen for later use.

1. Preheat oven to 375° and line a sheet pan with foil.
2. Cut the pumpkin in half and scoop out the seeds. Cut larger pumpkins/ squash into quarters.
3. Bake the pumpkin pieces for 40 to 60 minutes. Remove them from the oven when the flesh is soft. The edges may begin to brown, but do not allow to burn.
4. Once the pumpkin has cooled enough to handle, scoop out the flesh.
5. Seminole pumpkins tend to contain more water than traditional pie pumpkins or other hard squashes, however this may be a necessary step for traditional pumpkin as well. If it looks watery, remove the excess moisture by squeezing it in cheesecloth and letting it sit for 5 to 10 minutes to allow the moisture to run out. This is important for your pie filling to ensure that it sets properly.
6. Using an immersion blender or food processor, puree the drained pumpkin until it is smooth. The final texture should be thick and hold its shape when scooped out with a spoon.

SIMPLE FLAKY PIE CRUST

Ingredients:
- 1 ¼ cups all-purpose flour
- ¼ tsp salt
- ½ cup shortening, chilled OR ¼ cup shortening & ¼ cup cold unsalted butter- this is more finicky but also more flavorful.
- 3 Tbsp ice water

Directions:

1. In a medium bowl whisk the flour and salt together. With a pastry blender or fork, cut in the cold shortening and/ or butter until the mixture resembles coarse crumbs. Drizzle 2-3 Tbsp ice water over the flour. Toss mixture with the fork to moisten, adding more water a few drops at a time until the dough comes together.
2. Gently gather dough together into a ball, wrap in plastic wrap and chill for at least 30 minutes before rolling.
3. Roll out dough to about ¼ inch thickness and press into pie plate. Take care to not overwork the dough, this will cause it to become tough instead of flaky. Fill and/ or bake per pie instructions.

Bourbon Caramel Bread Pudding

This rich and decadent dessert combines the comforting classic of bread pudding with the sophisticated flavors of bourbon and caramel. This creamy vanilla infused custard bakes into a golden, tender pudding that is draped in buttery caramel sauce. It creates an unforgettable grand finale to any meal.

Ingredients
For the bread pudding:
- 10 cups brioche bread, cubed
- 3 cups heavy cream
- 2 cups milk
- 5 eggs
- 1 cup packed dark brown sugar
- 3 Tbsp bourbon
- 1 Tbsp vanilla bean paste or 1 whole vanilla bean, split lengthwise and beans scraped
- 1 tsp cinnamon
- ⅓ tsp grated nutmeg
- dash salt

For the sauce:
- 1 ½ cups unsalted butter
- 2 cups packed dark brown sugar
- 2 Tbsp bourbon
- 1 cup heavy cream
- 1 Tbsp vanilla bean paste
- 1 tsp cinnamon
- dash salt

Directions for the bread pudding:

1. Lightly coat a 13x9-inch baking dish with nonstick spray and arrange the brioche evenly.
2. In a large bowl whisk together all other ingredients to fully combine. Pour over the bread, tossing gently to make sure it is all fully coated. Let this sit for 1 hour so that the bread can full absorb the custard mixture.
3. Preheat the oven to 350° and bake for 50 minutes, or until puffy and set.
4. While baking, prepare the caramel sauce.

Directions for the sauce:

1. Melt the butter in a small saucepan over medium heat. Add the brown sugar and stir until fully dissolved and the mixture is bubbly. Remove from heat.
2. Stir in bourbon, cream, and vanilla. Return to heat and bring to a boil. Boil for 2 minutes.
3. Remove from heat and stir in salt and cinnamon.
4. To serve, drizzle sauce over bread pudding.

Sweet Potato Creme Brulee

Sweet potato is a staple for any harvest meal in both sweet and savory applications, so why not add it to the dessert menu as well? This unique take on traditional creme brulee takes the delectable vegetable and turns it into a silky-smooth custardy confection that dreams are made of!

Ingredients:
- 1 lb. sweet potatoes, peeled
- 3 ¾ cups heavy cream
- 3 ¾ cups milk
- 1 Tbsp cinnamon
- 1 Tbsp grated nutmeg
- 1 ½ tsp allspice
- 1 tsp salt
- 13 egg yolks
- 1 ½ cups sugar, plus extra for finishing

Directions:

1. Preheat the oven to 425°. Pierce whole sweet potatoes with a fork and place on a baking sheet. Bake for approximately 45 minutes and remove to cool, dicing when cool enough to handle. This can easily be done days ahead of time.
2. In a heavy saucepan combine cooked sweet potato, heavy cream, milk, and spices. Bring just to a boil then remove from heat and set aside.
3. In a separate bowl, whisk egg yolks and sugar together until light and creamy.
4. Drizzle a small amount of warm dairy mixture into the sugar/ yolk mixture, whisking constantly. This will raise the temperature slowly and prevent the egg yolks from cooking when added into the dairy.
5. Add the warmed egg mixture into the dairy, whisking constantly. Once fully combined, use an immersion blender to puree the mixture until smooth. Place in refrigerator to cool.
6. Lower oven temperature to 300°. Ladle custard mixture into individual ramekins or one large shallow ramekin and place in the middle of a baking dish.
7. Place on oven rack and create a water bath- pour enough water into the baking dish to reach at least halfway up the sides of the ramekins.
8. Bake for 20 to 30 minutes, until custard is set. Place in refrigerator to cool.
9. Just before serving, add a thin layer of sugar to the top and torch to create that iconic sugar shell.

Peanut Butter Buckeyes

This may be the first confection that I ever made when I was first married. As a born and raised Floridian, I didn't have a clue what my Ohio bred husband was talking about when he said he wanted me to make Buckeyes... a peanut butter ball dipped in chocolate to make it look like a nut?? I totally thought he was joking at first, but it sounded good, so I went to work researching and experimenting. And here we are, with a sweet little ball of goodness that tastes like a homemade Reeses cup and looks like a nut!

My baking tips: it's really important to scrape the bowl down after adding the powdered sugar to get it properly Incorporated. You don't want to end up with the top being super firm but then everything in the bottom being super soft.

Coconut oil helps thin the chocolate so it's easier to dip, but you can use shortening or vegetable oil if that's what you have on hand. Start with a small amount of oil to reach the dipping consistency that you want- remember you can always add more but you can't take away.

The butter can be adjusted +/- a tablespoon for a softer or firmer ball if desired.

Ingredients:
- 1 cup smooth peanut butter, not natural
- 6 Tbsp unsalted butter
- 2 ¼ cups powdered sugar, sifted, plus more if needed
- 1 tsp vanilla
- pinch salt
- 2 cups semisweet chocolate (melting wafers or chips)
- 2 Tbsp coconut oil

Directions:

1. In the bowl of a stand mixer fitted with the paddle attachment, cream together the peanut butter, butter, salt, and vanilla.
2. Slowly add the powdered sugar until you get a smooth consistency, stopping to scrape down the sides of the bowl occasionally. Mixture will be thick, with a consistency similar to play-dough.
3. Chill the mixture in the refrigerator for at least 30 minutes.
4. Line a baking sheet with parchment paper. Portion the peanut butter mixture out with a one tablespoon scoop and roll into balls. Place them on the baking sheet and chill until firm, about 20-30 minutes.
5. Meanwhile, add chocolate and coconut oil to a medium bowl and melt on 50% power in the microwave. Stir to combine and set aside to cool to room temperature.
6. Use a skewer or toothpick to dip the peanut butter

balls into the chocolate. Leave a bit of the peanut butter exposed for that signature buckeye look.

7. Chill to allow the chocolate to firm up and enjoy. If you want to remove the holes left from the skewers, run a small knife or spatula over the tops.

These will keep covered in the fridge for up to two weeks.

Cranberry Bars

This simple dessert began for me as a way to use leftover homemade cranberry sauce. It quickly became a reason to double the cranberry sauce recipe and is requested every year for family gatherings. I love its simplicity, and the fact that it comes together quickly and easily with no fuss. It hits all the right notes- sweet but not too sweet, a little tart, and just a little nutty.

Ingredients:
- 2 cups cranberry sauce
- 1 box yellow cake mix
- ¾ cups butter, melted
- 2 eggs
- 1 cup rolled oats
- ¾ cup dark brown sugar, packed
- 1 tsp ground ginger
- 1 tsp cinnamon

Directions:

1. Preheat oven to 350° and lightly grease a 9x 13-inch baking dish.
2. In a large bowl, mix together the cake mix, butter, and eggs to combine. Stir in the oats, brown sugar and spices.
3. Evenly spread enough of the mixture onto the bottom of the dish to cover, pressing with your fingers to form a thin crust, going ½ way up the sides.
4. Spread the cranberry sauce over your crust, going all the way to the edges.
5. Pinch off pieces of the remaining oat/ crust mixture and dot across the cranberry mixture.
6. Bake for 35-40 minutes, until the top is lightly browned. Cool completely before cutting into bars.

Mimosa Butter Cookies

Infused with the bright citrusy essence of orange and a subtle hint of champagne, this delicate butter cookie melts in your mouth. It's the perfect treat to serve with a classic Mimosa and elevate any brunch or special occasion.

Ingredients:
- 1 cup unsalted butter, softened
- 1 ¼ cup confectioners sugar, sifted
- zest of 2 oranges
- ½ tsp salt
- ¼ cup orange juice, approx. 1 orange juiced
- ¼ cup sparkling wine, sparkling cider, or sparkling white grape juice
- 2 ½ cup all-purpose flour

Directions:

1. Preheat oven to 350° and line a baking sheet with parchment. Do not grease or spray with cooking spray.

2. With a stand or hand mixer cream butter, confectioners sugar, zest, and salt until light and fluffy, about 3-5 minutes.
3. Combine juice and sparkling wine.
4. Alternating between flour and juice mixtures, add them into the butter/ sugar mixture ½ at a time; beating well and scraping down the sides of the bowl after each addition.
5. Refrigerating the dough at this point will help to give a more defined shape to your cookie, but is not necessary for flavor or texture purposes.
6. Cut a small hole in the tip of a pastry bag and insert a star tip, transfer dough to bag.
7. Pipe into circles or desired shape directly onto prepared baking sheet, 2 inches apart.
8. Bake for 10-12 minutes, until edges are set. Allow to cool on baking sheet.

Blood Orange Olive Oil Cake

Light and simple, this delicate cake is a moist and fragrant dessert that won't weigh you down at the end of a meal. The olive oil contributes a subtle fruitiness and a tender crumb, making each bite rich yet surprisingly light. This elegant cake offers a sophisticated flavor profile that is both comforting and refreshingly unique.

Ingredients:
- zest and juice of one blood orange or desired orange variety, you will need 1/3 cup juice
- 1 cup sugar
- 2 large eggs, room temperature
- ⅓ cup buttermilk
- ½ tsp vanilla bean paste
- ½ tsp. almond extract
- 1 ¾ cups all-purpose flour
- 1 ¼ tsp baking powder
- ¼ tsp baking soda
- ½ tsp salt
- ⅔ cups extra virgin olive oil

Directions:

1. Preheat the oven to 350° Grease and line a springform pan with parchment paper.
2. In a large mixing bowl whisk together zest, sugar, eggs, orange juice, buttermilk, vanilla, and almond extract together.
3. In a separate bowl sift together the flower, baking powder, baking soda, and salt.
4. Add the dry to the wet ingredients and mixed just until combined.
5. Gently fold in the olive oil just until combined.
6. Transfer the batter to prepared pan, bake for 30 to 35 minutes, until a toothpick inserted in the center comes out clean.

Apple Brownies

Rich gooey chocolatey brownies with a dash of warm fall spice and studded with tart apple bits and crunchy nuts blend together to create the perfect decadent treat that's impossible to resist.

Ingredients:
- 1 cup unsalted butter
- 2 ¼ cups sugar
- 1 ¼ cups Dutch processed cocoa powder
- 1 tsp baking powder
- 1 tsp salt
- 2 tsp cinnamon
- 1 Tbsp vanilla extract
- 4 large eggs, room temperature
- 1 ½ cups all-purpose flour
- 2 cups Granny Smith or other baking apple, peeled and diced
- ¾ cup pecans or walnuts, optional

Directions:

1. Preheat the oven to 350° Grease a 9x13-inch baking dish and set aside.
2. Melt butter in a saucepan over medium heat. Add the sugar and stir to combine. Stirring frequently, cook until all the sugar is dissolved and the mixture becomes glossy.
3. In a mixing bowl whisk together the cocoa, baking powder, salt, and cinnamon.
4. Whisk in the sugar mixture, eggs, and vanilla, mixing until smooth.
5. Add the flour and nuts if using, stir until smooth. Gently fold in the apples.
6. Pour batter into the prepared baking dish, bake for 30 to 35 minutes. Allow to cool before cutting.

Butterscotch Pie

Golden, mile-high meringue with its perfectly toasted peaks, sit atop a creamy, rich butterscotch filling, instantly transporting you to grandmother's kitchen on a Sunday afternoon. Each bite of the smooth, sweet butterscotch against the airy, crisp meringue is a delicious reminder of holiday gatherings and the warmth of family laughter. This pie isn't just a dessert; it's a comforting hug, baked with love and brimming with nostalgic flavors that taste like home.

Ingredients:
Pie:
- 9-inch pie crust, homemade or store bought* see recipe for simple flaky pie crust
- ¼ cup unsalted butter
- 1 cup dark brown sugar, packed
- 4 Tbsp all-purpose flour
- 2 cups whole milk
- 3 large egg yolks, reserve whites for meringue
- 1 tsp vanilla bean paste
- pinch salt

Meringue:
- 3 egg whites, reserved from above
- 1 tsp vanilla bean paste
- ¼ tsp cream of tartar
- 6 Tbsp sugar

Direction:

1. Preheat oven to 350°, and fully bake pie crust.
2. In a heavy saucepan over medium heat melt butter and add brown sugar, stir frequently until sugar is dissolved, then cook 2-3 minutes longer and remove from heat.
3. In a large mixing bowl, combine flour with ½ of the milk and mix until smooth. Add egg yolks and salt and mix well. Blend in remaining milk.
4. Add flour mixture to saucepan with sugar/ butter and cook on medium low heat until thickened, stirring CONSTANTLY. This can take anywhere from 30-45 minutes. Do not raise heat or rush this process as it will develop a burnt taste.
5. Remove from heat and stir in vanilla, pour into fully baked pie crust.
6. To make meringue: with a stand or hand mixer, beat egg whites with cream of tartar until soft peaks form. Add vanilla. Gradually add sugar, beating until stiff and glossy peaks form and all sugar is dissolved.
7. Spread meringue over slightly warm filling, sealing to edge of crust.
8. Bake for 12-15 minutes, or until meringue is golden. Cool before serving and store in refrigerator.

Debbie's Chocolate Delight

In our family Chocolate Delight means home, time spent with family, and love. I don't know where the original recipe came from, most likely a community or church cookbook from long ago. What I do know is that it is now a treasured recipe that will be passed on for many generations to come. Because when it comes to family traditions it's not about how fancy the recipe is or how long it takes to make, it's about the memories that it invokes. I hope that our family's delight brings you as much joy as it has for us. And THAT'S the best way to end a meal.

Ingredients:
Crust:
- 1 stick unsalted butter, melted
- 1 cup flour, sifted
- 2 Tbsp sugar
- ¼ tsp salt
- 1 tsp vanilla extract
- 1 cup chopped pecans

Filling:

- 1 cup confectioners sugar
- 1 8 oz package cream cheese, softened
- 16 oz cool whip, divided
- 2 pkg instant chocolate pudding mix
- 3 cups milk
- chocolate shavings for garnish

Directions:

1. Preheat oven to 300°, grease a 9x13-inch baking dish.
2. Mix all crust ingredients until fully combined. Press into the bottom of the prepared baking dish and bake for 20-30 minutes until lightly browned. Cool completely before filling.
3. While the crust bakes, you will make 2 separate filling mixtures.
4. Combine confectioners sugar, cream cheese, and ½ the cool whip and set aside.
5. With a hand mixer or immersion blender mix pudding mix with milk, set aside.
6. To assemble, evenly spread the cream cheese mixture over the cooled crust. Pour the pudding mixture over that and spread evenly. Finally cover the top with remaining cool whip.
7. Garnish with chocolate shavings.

Part Six

Drinks and Cozy Beverages- Sips of Comfort

Who doesn't love wrapping their hands around a steaming mug of spiced cider or creamy hot chocolate at the end of a day? Or that first sip of a cozy cocktail with good friends? These aren't just concoctions; they're liquid comforts designed to complete that perfect occasion. Whether you're curled up with a good book, enjoying a quiet moment, or sharing laughter with loved ones, a perfect sip can bring that distinctive Autumn glow and sweet contentment right into your cup.

MY COCKTAIL TIPS:

Whether you're simmering cider on the stove or crafting a frosty Autumn cocktail, the secret to truly unforgettable drinks lies in the attention to flavor. For hot beverages, resist the urge to rush; allowing ingredients like whole spices or cocoa powder to gently warm and mingle over low heat helps their flavors to become deep and rich. And for blended sips, fresh quality ingredients are always best. Here, blending just enough to combine everything is the difference between overdiluted and watery and a cocktail that's bursting with beautifully developed flavors.

Classic Hot Apple Cider

If you've never tried apple cider made from scratch, it's a must do this fall. It's so much fresher (not to mention healthier, with much less added sugar) than anything that you could buy at the store, and so easy to do. Not to mention that your house will smell amazing. And bonus points, you can make the best homemade applesauce or apple butter with the cooked apple.

My cocktail tips: Make extra to have on hand for all the lovely cocktails that you're going to make this fall season!

You can easily make this in the crock pot and let it simmer for 6-8 hours on low

For the best flavor balance use a blend of apple varieties, not just 1 type. I recommend using a mix of tart (like Granny Smith or McIntosh) and sweet (like Gala, Fuji, or Honeycrisp)

Add a little spice with an 1 inch piece of peeled ginger.

Ingredients:
- 10- 12 apples (assorted types) with skin on, quartered and cored, plus a few slices for garnish.

- 1 whole orange, peeled
- water to cover, anywhere from 12- 16 cups
- ½ cup brown sugar or maple syrup
- 4 cinnamon sticks or 2 tsp ground cinnamon
- 2 tsp whole or ½ tsp ground cloves
- ½ tsp freshly ground nutmeg
- 2 tsp ground allspice
- cinnamon sugar for rimming glass

Directions:

1. Put the apples and oranges into a large stock pot and cover with water, leaving a few inches of space at the top of the pot. Add the sugar and spices and bring to a boil.
2. Reduce heat to medium and cover, simmering for about 2 hours.
3. Mash the apples against the side of the pot to release more flavor and simmer for another hour.
4. Set a large fine mesh sieve over a bowl. scoop out the majority of the cooked down apples and transfer to the strainer (if you do not have fine mesh, try a standard colander lined with cheesecloth). Once the bulk of the solids are removed, pour the remaining liquid over them to strain. Gently press down on the cooked apple mixture to remove as much liquid as possible. You may have to repeat this process a second time depending on how well it strains
5. Serve warm in cinnamon sugar rimmed mugs or cool and store in an airtight container in the refrigerator.
6. Remove whole spices and reserve the cooked apple mixture for homemade applesauce or apple butter

(to use on your freshly made pumpkin scones or buttermilk biscuits!).

Chai Spiced Hot Tea Latte

A chai tea latte is a warm and comforting drink that combines spiced black tea with milk, often frothed, and a sweetener. There are many variations, from using pre-made chai concentrates to brewing your own chai from scratch with whole spices. This recipe focuses on keeping it homemade yet still simple.

MY COCKTAIL TIPS:

Spice Level: Adjust the spices to your preference. For a bolder flavor, you can increase the quantities or add black peppercorn.

Sweetness: Try a different sweetener and adjust the quantity.

Milk: Experiment with different types of milk. Whole milk gives a rich, creamy texture, while oat milk will be a little less creamy but is a great dairy-free alternative.

Iced Chai Latte: To make an iced version, let the chai

concentrate cool completely. Fill a glass with ice, pour in the cooled chai, and then add cold milk. Stir well.

Ingredients:
- 1 cup water
- 1-2 black tea bags, like English Breakfast or Darjeeling, or ½ Tbsp loose leaf black tea
- ½ tsp ground cinnamon, or 1 cinnamon stick
- ¼ tsp ground ginger, or a 1-inch piece of ginger, peeled
- ¼ tsp ground cardamom, or 1 cardamom pod
- pinch of ground cloves, or 2-3 whole cloves
- pinch of ground nutmeg
- honey, to taste
- 1 tsp vanilla
- ¾ - 1 cup whole, oat, or coconut milk

Directions:

1. In a small saucepan over medium high heat combine all the spices (cinnamon, ginger, cardamom, cloves, nutmeg) and toast them lightly until aromatic, about 3 minutes. Add the water and bring the mixture to a boil.
2. Reduce heat to low and simmer for 5-10 minutes to allow the flavors to meld and intensify.
3. Turn off the heat and add the tea bags or leaves. Cover and let steep for another 5-10 minutes.
4. If using whole spices or loose-leaf tea, strain the chai concentrate through a fine-mesh strainer into a mug, discarding the solids. If using only ground spices and tea bags, simply remove the tea bags.
5. Add honey and vanilla.

6. While the tea is steeping, heat the milk in a separate small saucepan over medium heat until it's hot and steaming, but not boiling. If you have a milk frother, froth the milk until it's foamy. If you don't have a frother, you can vigorously whisk the milk by hand while it's heating to create some foam.

7. Pour the frothed milk into your mug with the chai concentrate. Spoon any extra foam on top.

8. Sprinkle with a pinch of ground cinnamon or nutmeg for garnish.

Autumn Glow Green Tea with Spiced Pear and Ginger

This lovely tea is a delightful departure from the ordinary; offering a subtle sweetness from pears, a warming kick from ginger, and the delicate earthiness of green tea. I can see Nan Nettles curled up on the porch at sunset with a steaming mug and a warm blanket now.

Ingredients:
- 2 cups water
- 1 ripe firm pear, peeled, cored, and diced
- 1 inch piece of fresh ginger, peeled and thinly sliced or grated
- 1 cinnamon stick
- 3-4 whole cardamom pods, or ¼ tsp ground cardamom
- 2 green tea bags, or 2 tsp loose leaf green tea in a diffuser
- 1-2 tsp honey, to taste
- squeeze of lemon juice, optional

Directions:

1. In a small saucepan, combine the water, diced pear, sliced ginger, and spices.
2. Bring to a gentle simmer over medium heat, reduce the heat to low, cover and let simmer for 10-15 minutes. This allows the pear to soften slightly and all the spices to release their aromatic oils into the water.
3. Remove from the heat and add the tea bags or diffuser. Let steep for 2-3 minutes. Avoid over-steeping, as it can become bitter.
4. Remove tea bags/ diffuser and strain mixture through a fine mesh sieve, pressing the pear to extract all of the liquid.
5. Sweeten with honey or other sweetener and a squeeze of lemon juice as desired.

Butter Pecan Latté

It's taken me half my life, but I've only just begun to like coffee drinks. It's definitely been fueled by a need for caffeine and the plethora of coffee houses on every corner- each with their own unique takes on all the sugary, syrupy, concoctions full of cream, calories, and joy. This brought me to the realization that there must be a better way, without all the extra sugar and added expense. This beautifully easy and wonderfully creamy concoction is a perfect fall flavored pick me up that will definitely be in my rotation for many years to come.

Ingredients:
- 2 cups whole or oat milk
- 2 Tbsp dark brown sugar
- 1 tsp maple syrup
- 1 tsp butternut extract*
- ½ cup strong coffee or espresso
- whipped cream

*if you cannot find butternut (also called butter & nut extract), you can use a combination of vanilla, butter, and almond or hazelnut extracts

Directions:

1. In a small saucepan over medium heat whisk together the milk, brown sugar, maple sugar and extract until the sugars have dissolved and it begins to thicken. Do NOT boil. Froth the milk mixture with an immersion blender or frother.
2. Pour milk over coffee and top with whipped cream.

Frozen Coffee Hot Chocolate

It gets really hot in Florida, and I LOVE hot chocolate, but only really enjoy it for a few short months when it's not approx. 1000° outside. So, in my personal opinion, the person who had the idea to blend hot chocolate with ice was just sheer genius. Had to be a Floridian, right?? I've taken it a step further and added coffee, because iced coffee is also amazing so clearly, they need to be blended. As I like to say all the time, have fun with it and make it your own. Try adding hazelnut or almond extract, or a caramel drizzle, or for a wintery effect you could add peppermint extract and crumbles on top. The possibilities are as endless as your imagination!

Ingredients:
- 1 ½ cups whole or oat milk
- 2 Tbsp unsweetened cocoa powder
- 6 oz semi sweet baking chocolate
- ¼ cup honey or maple syrup
- 1-2 tsp vanilla extract
- 1 cup chilled brewed coffee
- 3-4 cups ice

- marshmallow fluff, whipped cream, chocolate syrup and/ or chocolate for garnish (grated, chopped or curls)

Directions:

1. In a small saucepan over medium heat whisk together the milk, cocoa powder, chocolate, honey or syrup, and vanilla, and bring to a simmer. Whisk continually until the chocolate is melted and ingredients are fully blended. Do NOT boil. Allow to cool completely.
2. Add coffee, cooled chocolate mixture, and 3 cups of ice to a blender. Blend until smooth, adding more ice if needed until you have reached desired consistency.
3. Pour into serving glass and top with your choice of garnish.

Pumpkin Pie Punch

This drink just IS fall. As soon as you take the first sip you are transported to a dreamy forest where the air is crisp and the colored leaves are falling all around you. There's probably pumpkins scattered about in all shapes and sizes, and a corn maze nearby. It's smooth and creamy, but also fizzy and light thanks to the ginger beer. No matter where you are, the sweet-spicy balance is guaranteed to warm you from your toes to your nose.

My cocktail tip: Make it kid friendly and non-alcoholic by leaving out the rum and increasing the amounts of apple cider and orange juice.

Ingredients:
- 1 ½ cups apple cider
- 1 cup orange juice
- ¼ cup lemon juice
- ½ cup pumpkin puree
- ½ cup maple syrup
- ½ cup bourbon spiced rum

- 2 tsp pumpkin pie spice
- ½ tsp ground cinnamon 2 cinnamon sticks
- ¼ tsp ground nutmeg
- 1 cup ginger beer
- apple slices, cinnamon sticks, and or orange slices for garnish

Directions:

1. In a large pitcher combine juices, pumpkin, and maple syrup, stirring to mix well and dissolve the syrup. Stir in rum.
2. Add the spices and again mix well until combined.
3. Serve over ice with a splash of ginger beer and garnish.

Autumn Citrus & Rosemary Spritzer

This festive fall cocktail highlights all the flavors of the season beautifully, creating a sophisticated and utterly delicious way to toast the cozier months.

Ingredients
For the rosemary simple syrup:
- ¼ cup sugar
- ¼ cup water
- 1 sprig fresh rosemary

For the spritzer:
- 2 oz blood orange juice or 1 fresh blood orange
- 2 oz apple cider
- Fresh rosemary leaves, about 6
- Juice of 1 lemon, approx. 2 oz
- 2 oz rosemary simple syrup
- 3 oz gin or vodka
- 4 oz orange sparkling water
- 2 sprigs of fresh rosemary for garnish

Directions:

1. To make the rosemary simple syrup add the sugar, water and rosemary sprig to a small saucepan. Bring to a simmer on medium low heat for about 5 minutes. Remove from heat and set aside to cool.
2. Add blood orange, apple cider, and rosemary leaves to the cocktail shaker and mash together. (muddle)
3. Add the lemon juice, simple syrup, gin or vodka, and ice and shake well.
4. Pour over fresh ice into 2 cocktail glasses and fill the rest of the way with sparkling water.
5. Garnish with a sprig of rosemary.

Cranberry Mulled White Wine

Perfect for any party or gathering, this warm mulled wine is a light, crisp variation of its classic red counterpart. It has tons of cozy appeal with all the notes of citrus, aromatic spices and earthy rosemary that you want from a warm fall mug.

Ingredients:
- 1 cup white cranberry juice, divided
- 2 sprigs fresh rosemary
- peel of 1 lime or orange, being careful to not include any white pith
- 1 bottle dry white wine, such as Chardonnay, Sauvignon Blanc or Pinot Grigio
- 1 cup fresh or frozen cranberries, thawed
- 2 cinnamon sticks
- 2 star anise
- 5 whole cloves
- ⅓ cup honey, if desired
- ¼ cup light rum

Directions:

1. In a heavy saucepan, combine ½ cup of cranberry juice and sprigs of rosemary. Bring to a boil and simmer for approx. 3 minutes, remove rosemary.
2. Add lime or orange peel, remaining cranberry juice, wine, and spices. Cook on low heat for 1 hour, until warm and flavors are blended through.
3. Strain with a fine mesh sieve and stir in rum and honey if desired.
4. Serve warm with garnishes of rosemary, cranberries, and cinnamon sticks.

Honey Grapefruit Bellini

This bubbly cocktail beautifully marries the vibrant tang of fresh seasonal grapefruit with the cozy sweetness of honey, creating a sophisticated yet approachable sip that's perfect for a festive brunch or a romantic evening by the fire with a special someone.

My cocktail tips: Simple syrups are widely used in all sorts of drinks and can be as simple as the honey syrup here or have many other flavors added, but it always starts with a 1:1 ratio of water and any form of sweetener. Have fun and experiment with added flavors and make extra to sweeten your morning coffee or tea with!

Ingredients:
- 1 large grapefruit
- 1-2 Tbsp honey syrup, to taste
- chilled Prosecco or Champagne

Directions:

1. Create a honey syrup by adding equal parts honey and water to a small saucepan and heating until the honey is fully melted. Simmer for a few minutes more and set aside to cool.
2. Peel the grapefruit, removing all white pith. Make sure at least some of the peel is in strips to use as garnish later, set those aside for now.
3. Roughly chop the segments and remove any seeds. In a blender, blend the grapefruit flesh until very smooth- you may need a splash of water to get it moving. Strain through a fine mesh sieve if you prefer a smoother, pulp free puree.
4. Sweeten the grapefruit puree with 1-2 Tbsp of honey syrup. Taste and adjust sweetness as needed.
5. Spoon about 2 oz of the sweetened grapefruit puree into the bottom of a chilled champagne flute. Slowly top with chilled prosecco or champagne, allowing the bubbles to mix with the puree.
6. Stir gently if needed to combine and garnish with a grapefruit twist and sprig of mint.

Spiced Fall Sangria

Embrace the bounty of the season with crisp apples, juicy pears and more with a symphony of aromatic spices and a touch of sweetness. Make a big pitcher to share during this season of gathering with friends and family, because it's as delicious to sip on as it is beautiful to look at.

Ingredients:
- 2 cups spiced apple cider
- 1 bottle of your favorite wine, white or red
- ½ cup brandy, bourbon, or cinnamon whiskey
- 1 ½ cups pomegranate arils
- 2 apples, any variety- try a mix of Honeycrisp and Granny Smith, diced
- 2 pears, diced
- 2 plums, diced
- 1 star fruit, sliced
- ½ cup grapes, halved
- 2 cinnamon sticks
- cranberry ginger ale, as desired
- maple syrup and cinnamon sugar for garnish

Directions:

1. Place prepared fruits and cinnamon sticks in a large pitcher. Add in cider, wine and brandy or whiskey and stir to combine.
2. Refrigerate for at least 2 hours or overnight.
3. Just before serving, rim each glass with maple syrup and cinnamon sugar.
4. Scoop some of the fruit into each glass before pouring and top off with cranberry ginger ale for sparkling effect.

Pumpkin Spice Martini

Creamy, sweet, and bursting with all the flavors of a pumpkin pie, this delectable martini is a great seasonal twist on the classic that will have you saying "cheers" to fall in no time. Get ready to shake up some seasonal martini magic.

Ingredients:
- 1 ½ oz vanilla vodka
- 1 ½ oz Irish cream liqueur
- 1 ½ oz pumpkin liqueur
- If you can't find pumpkin liqueur:
- 1 ½ Tbsp pumpkin puree
- ¼ tsp pumpkin pie spice
- splash of maple syrup
- ice
- For garnish: ground cinnamon and/or nutmeg, whipped cream, cinnamon stick
- For rimming glass: graham cracker crumbs, sugar, pumpkin pie spice

Directions:

Prepare your glass:

1. In a small dish combine finely crushed graham crackers with a pinch of pumpkin pie spice and sugar.
2. Dip the rim of your martini glass into a bit of Irish cream liqueur or maple syrup, then gently roll it in the graham cracker mixture until coated.
3. Place the rimmed glass in the freezer to chill while you prepare the drink.

Prepare the drink:

1. Fill a cocktail shaker with ice.
2. Pour in the vodka, Irish cream, and pumpkin liqueurs (or pumpkin puree/ spice mixture)
3. Securely close the shaker lid and shake vigorously for at least 15-30 seconds, or until the outside of the shaker is frosty. This will ensure that the ingredients are well chilled and blended.
4. Strain into your chilled, rimmed martini glass.
5. Garnish with a dollop of whipped cream, a sprinkle of ground cinnamon, and a cinnamon stick.

Crown Royal Caramel Apple Cocktail

Who needs to go bobbing for apples when Crown has given us the gift of their Apple Whiskey!! I can't imagine what pairs better than rich creamy caramel with this smooth blend of apple and whiskey, so curl up in your coziest blanket and get ready to enjoy this perfectly autumn treat.

My cocktail tips: You could also try the Salted Caramel Whiskey for more caramel and less apple flavor or do ½ & ½. And try a little dash of cinnamon as an added garnish

Ingredients:
- 2 tsp caramel sauce + more for rim of glass
- 2 oz Crown Royal Apple Whiskey
- 3 oz apple cider
- 1 ½ oz ginger ale
- brown sugar & cinnamon stick for garnish

Directions:

1. Rim your cocktail glass by dipping the edge in caramel syrup and then brown sugar.
2. Add the 2 tsp caramel sauce to the bottom of the glass.
3. Pour Crown Apple Whiskey over the caramel sauce and stir until the caramel has fully dissolved.
4. Add apple cider and stir well to combine.
5. Add ice and top with ginger ale.

Coming Next Spring

Coming next spring: Daffodil and Devon Scones

As Nan's 70th birthday approaches, a strange melody drifts down from the attic, wrapping the Nettles B&B in a dreamy hush. Guests begin to nod off mid-sentence, and even the ghosts are unusually quiet. Meanwhile, Mossy is up to something in the garden—something involving tarps, tools, and far too much secrecy.

With spring in full bloom and magic in the air, Nan and Mossy find themselves tangled in another haunting mystery. And this time, the enchantment has strings attached.

Also by Chrissy Chicory

Volume 4: The Art of Play

Chrissy Chicory's fiction and nonfiction books are available through Amazon, Apple Books, Barnes & Noble, Kobo, and other major eBook and print retailers—plus library services like OverDrive, Hoopla, and Scribd through Draft2Digital's wide distribution.

The Ink and Verse handwriting series is currently available exclusively on Amazon.

About Chrissy Chicory

Chrissy Chicory is a Florida author known for her enchanting blend of magic, heart, and literary whimsy. Her stories wrap readers in cozy mysteries, poetic romantasy, and gentle inspiration—each one a love letter to the power of imagination.

In *The Culebra Chronicles*, Chrissy brings the historic streets of St. Augustine to life through the eyes of a group of magical half-fae sisters. Blending supernatural suspense with romantasy and Florida folklore, the series follows their journey through ghost tours, pirate curses, and long-buried family secrets—beginning with *Unabashedly Chosen* and deepening with each revelation.

The *Nettles B&B Paracozy Series* showcases her flair for haunted heirlooms, meddling pixies, and unexpected second chances. Set in a lovingly restored Victorian bed-and-breakfast on the Florida coast, the series is full of charm, mystery, and just the right amount of sticky buns. *Mums and Pumpkin Pie* is the third novel in this growing series.

Beyond fiction, Chrissy's *Ink and Verse* series celebrates the art of handwriting with penmanship workbooks inspired by the world's greatest poets—offering a meditative way to slow down and connect with beauty.

Her *Lucid Living* series explores mindfulness, self-discovery, and gentle personal development. With reflection prompts and poetic encouragement, each book is a soft invitation to live with greater intention and grace.

Chrissy's books offer a comforting escape into the magical corners of everyday life. With each new release, she invites readers to sip some tea, light a candle, and step into stories where wonder waits around every page.

Sign up for Chrissy's cozy newsletter at ChrissyChicory.com and receive free ebook prequels—*Lilac and Cherry Tarts* (Nettles B&B), *Eternally Connected* (Culebra Chronicles), and a sample poem to copy out from her handwriting series, *Ink and Verse*.

Chrissy also hosts *The Velvet Teacup Society*, a reader group devoted to cozy magic, monthly teacup giveaways, and virtual pajama tea parties.
Join the fun at ChrissyChicory.com/Velvet-Teacup-Society

Magic is all around us.

About Teresa Sebring

Teresa Sebring is a Cordon Bleu–trained cook with a heart rooted in seasonal flavors and family traditions. She believes the kitchen is the warmest place in any home—and that food made with care is one of the most enduring ways to say "I love you."

Whether she's working with garden herbs, farmers market finds, or a forgotten family recipe, Teresa delights in turning simple ingredients into something memorable. This is her first cookbook, lovingly inspired by the belief that cooking isn't just a skill—it's a love language.

She lives in Florida with a house full of animals, the joyful chaos of family, and the delicious scent of something always baking.

A Kindly Word from the Hosts

Thank you so much for spending time with us at the Nettles B&B.

We hope the mums were in bloom, the pumpkin pie was perfectly spiced,

and the mystery left you feeling just the right amount of enchanted.

If you enjoyed your stay, we'd be ever so grateful if you left a short review.

Even a few kind words help other curious guests find their way to our little corner of the world.

Think of it as a cinnamon-sprinkled note tucked into the recipe box —or a cozy candle lit in the window.

With heartfelt thanks,

Nan (and Mossy, who would like to add...)

"A story shared is like a pie sliced—

meant to be savored and passed around."

—Mossy Nettles

You can leave a review where you purchased your book—or wherever you enjoy sharing cozy magic with fellow readers.

Thank you for reading—

may your kettle always sing, your crusts stay golden,

and may the pixies behave... at least until dessert.

www.ingramcontent.com/pod-product-compliance
Lightning Source LLC
Chambersburg PA
CBHW050923030726
47503CB00007BB/2433